"To be frank, I thought of the whole thing as a kind of joke. Earth—how can it exist? It's the same as Bonanza and Jackpot and Eden and all the rest. A name given to a dream of eternal happiness. You must have heard the stories, Earl. The legends. The world on which there is no pain or hurt or fear. The trees grow food of all descriptions, the rivers are wine, the very air is a perfumed caress. The sun never burns, the nights never chill, garments are made as needed from leaves and flowers.

"The concept is intoxicating and we became drunk on wild hopes and fantastic optimism. To find Earth. To dip our hands in its inexhaustible treasure. To cure all our ills and slake all our desires. Paradise!"

World of Promise

O

E. C. Tubb

DAW Books, Inc.
Donald A. Wollheim, Publisher

1633 Broadway, New York, N.Y. 10019

DEDICATION

To Phil and Doreen Rodgers

FIRST PRINTING, NOVEMBER 1980

1 2 3 4 5 6 7 8 9

DAW TRADEMARK REGISTERED
U.S. PAT. OFF. MARCA
REGISTRADA. HECHO EN U.S.A.

PRINTED IN U.S.A.

Chapter One

Against the tawdry velvet the dolls were things of enchantment: bright shapes of tinsel and glitter with hair of various hues formed into elaborate coiffures, eyes like gems, limbs and bodies traced with glowing colors, sparkling with sequins, stuffed with aromatic herbs.

"Mummy!" The voice was thin, high, crackling with childish longing. "Look, Mummy! Please may I have one?"

"No, child."

"Please, Mummy! Please!"

"No, Lavinia! Don't ask again!"

Dumarest turned, seeing the small figure at his side, the mane of hair which formed an ebon waterfall over the narrow shoulders—a frame for the rounded, piquant face, the widely spaced eyes now filled with a hopeless yearning. One which matched that of the woman who blinked as she forced herself to be harsh.

She said, as if conscious of his presence, "You know we can't afford to buy such things, child. Later, when we get back home, I'll make you one. I promise."

A promise she would keep at the cost of lost sleep and small comforts, but it wouldn't be the same. She lacked the skill to produce such false beauty and nothing could ever replace the magic of this special moment. Behind her a man, thick-set, dressed in rough and patched clothing, coughed and fumbled in a pocket.

"Maybe we could manage, Floria, if—"

"No, Roy!" The need to refuse accentuated her sharpness. "Bran needs all we can give him." She looked at the robed figure standing at the man's side. "He must be given his chance."

Determination must have driven them for years and Dumarest could guess at the sacrifices they had made. The man, a farmer he guessed, was decades younger than he looked, the woman the same. The youth, shapeless in his dun-colored robe, stood with a listless detachment, the face masked by the raised cowl pale, the eyes bruised with chronic fatigue. A family cursed by endless study and endless economies so that one of them, at least, would gain the chance to better himself.

But must the girl also pay?

Dumarest stooped and closed his hands about the small waist and lifted the girl high to sit on his shoulder. As the man opened his mouth to protest, he said, quickly, "With your permission, sir. I have my reasons. Allow me to buy your daughter a doll."

"But—"

"Roy!" The woman closed her hand on his arm. "No, husband!"

"He offers charity—"

"No!" With a woman's quick intuition she sensed it was more than that. Sensed too that Dumarest would not be denied. Her voice fell, became a whisper as, ignoring her, he concentrated on the child.

"Choose," he urged. "Take your time and pick which one you want."

She needed no time—the decision had been made already. Her hand lifted, the finger steady as it aimed at the second largest.

"That one." Her tone was wistful. "Please, may I have that one?"

"A wise choice." The vendor had remained silent knowing that to press too soon was to risk losing the sale. Now she came forward, smiling, smoothing the scarlet hair of the doll as she lifted it from its place. "The finest materials and skills have gone into the fabrication of this product. Note the eyes and the way they seem to move as you turn them against the light. The hair can be washed and set in a variety of styles. The face is capable of slight alteration, see?" The cheeks developed hollows beneath the pressure of her fingers, smoothed as she manipulated the plastic. "And the stuffing will retain its potency for years, bringing comfort and tranquility and restful sleep."

Valued comforts on any world and to be envied on Podesta.

Dumarest nodded, swung the girl from his shoulder, straightened to face the vendor who still held the doll.

"How much?"

The price had been decided as the child had made her choice. The family were poor and Dumarest wore a student's robe to match that of the youth but their poverty need not be mutual. A man studying for a whim, a noble paying a forfeit, a rich man amusing himself—such were not uncommon at the fair. But the vendor had seen his face and had abandoned the hope of an inflated profit. Here was no gull to be cheated.

"Fifteen corlms, my lord." As she picked up the coins she added, mechanically, "Good luck attend your studies."

"I'll echo that." Roy cleared his throat, aware of his previous antagonism and embarrassed by it. "I thought you were taking pity on us at first, but Floria explained. A superstition, I understand. Well, I'm no man to deny another his search for luck. You're for Ascelius, I see. Just like Bran here." He nodded at his son. "I've got him passage on the *Evidia*—fifth class, hard but cheap." Then, as Dumarest made no comment, he coughed and ended, "Well, I just wanted to thank you. We all did."

The woman, with her quick wit and the facile lie which had saved her husband's pride, now as Dumarest extended the doll to the child, said quickly, "Don't snatch it, Lavinia. Thank the gentleman properly."

"How can I, Mummy?"

"You'll have to kneel," she said to Dumarest. "Allow her to kiss you."

For a moment he hesitated, looking at the woman, reading the understanding in her eyes. Then he knelt, the doll in one hand, arms extended as the child ran into their embrace.

7

"Thank you," she whispered. "Thank you for the doll."

Then she was warm and soft against him, the touch of her lips moist on his cheek, small hands at his shoulders. A timeless instant which shattered as he rose to stand above her, the silken smoothness of her hair a memory against his palm—a moment she had already forgotten, engrossed as she was with her new toy.

The wind had turned fitful, gusting from the town and blowing over the field, the clustered booths of the fair, catching the rising columns of colored smoke and stinging his eyes with drifting acridity.

Blinking, Dumarest took shelter in an open-fronted tent, buying a mug of spiced tisane, sipping it as he looked over the area. The crowds had thickened as had the noise, and both would increase as the night grew older, not easing until the dawn, not ending until the closing of the fair two days from now. A misnomer—the fair was only called that because of the entrepreneurs taking advantage of the occasion; the vendors and touts, the harlots and gamblers, clowns, tumblers, freaks, the sellers of dreams and builders of hope, the merchants and traders and caterers to vice and pleasure who moved from world to world adding color and gaiety to a host of gatherings, living like transient parasites on the events of time.

"A word in your ear, sir." The man standing beside Dumarest looked cautiously from side to side. "But first your promise that our discourse will remain confidential. I have it?"

Dumarest sipped at his tisane.

"A man of discretion," applauded the stranger. "One who knows that silence is a message within itself. Now, sir, to be frank, I find myself in an invidious position. My client—I am an investigator—has died. The assignment he gave me was to obtain for him certain information regarding an examination held before the granting of a degree of special merit on a world which need not be named at this time. Passing the examination and gaining the degree offers great financial and academic advantages. The cost of obtaining the information—to be frank, the answers to the questions—was considerable and, as I mentioned, my client died before I could be recompensed. You understand the situation?"

"I think so." Dumarest looked into his mug. "You want to sell me the answers to the examination questions?"

"You put it bluntly, sir, but you have grasped the point. Such an intelligence does not shame the robe you wear. Now, as a student, you will appreciate the opportunity I offer. Copied, the information will make you financially independent, and a few sales will recoup the initial outlay."

"I'm not interested."

"You should be." The man had a thin, avian face, the eyes hooded, the mouth pursed. "Need I remind you that education does not come cheap? That to fail an examination could mean the loss of years of effort? Isn't it logical to take all precautions against that happening?"

Dumarest said flatly, "I told you I'm not interested. You're wasting your time. Now just move on and stop bothering me."

He finished the tisane as the stranger moved away in search of a more gullible victim. He could even find one; some scared and timid youth desperate at the thought of failure and willing to buy an imagined security. More likely the relative of a student would fall for his lies and hand the expensive rubbish over as a final gift. In either case both would have paid for their folly.

Setting down the empty mug, Dumarest moved from the tent and paused on the wide path running between the facing booths. Between two of them he could see the area beyond; more open, thronged now with little groups, studded with stands selling drinks, comestibles, gaudy confections. A scene lit with the burning hues of torches set high on slender poles; chemical flares casting patches of somber browns, smoldering oranges, dusty blues, intense purples, vivid greens, burning yellows, savage reds. Circus colors augmented by the blaze of stars covering the sky in a myriad of glittering points, the sheets and curtains of luminescence, the silver glow of triple moons.

From somewhere down the midway came the thud of drums and a sudden burst of laughter; strained amusement too raucous to be genuine, sounds made to cover an aching grief, a fear, an anxiety grown too great. Those gathered had not come for the fun available but to make their farewells— all wearing the dun-colored robe would be taking ships for

Ascelius, the vessels themselves now ranked on the field or heading into orbit.

"Mister!" A woman called to him, her body moving with sinuous grace. "A lecture hall can be a dull place—why not take a little pleasure while you can? Come with me and taste the realities of life. For ten corlms I will teach you a new art. For twenty I will stun your senses. For fifty I will give you paradise."

She shrugged as he moved on, knowing better than to scream insults, knowing such actions could bring an ugly return. And why waste time on one when others were available?

Dumarest heard her make a fresh offer as he slipped between two booths and into the open area. His ship was on the field, his passage booked, but for reasons of his own he delayed boarding. Instead he walked to where a throng had gathered around an area bright with unexpected light. The crowd had formed a circle, faces turned like sun-loving flowers toward the illumination, eyes intent on what they saw.

A cage stood beneath suspended lights, a thing of stout bars and braces, wheeled for ease of transport, ringed with a handful of guards. In it paced a beast.

It was half again as tall as a man, twice as broad, the hands like spades, the fingers tipped with claws as were the toes of the splayed feet. The body was dark with thickly matted hair grown so close that it seemed the texture of horn. The face was a nightmare of jutting jaw, fangs, burning eyes and pointed ears. The plated skull bore two stubby horns, their tips glistening with metallic sharpness. The neck was as thick as the thighs, which were as thick as the waist of a woman.

"Look at it!" A man sucked in his breath as he spoke to the woman at his side. "How would you like to meet that in a dark alley?"

"I wouldn't." The sight which entranced him nauseated her. "Come away, Lou."

"You don't like it?"

"I think it's vile." She gave her reason. "It's too much like a man. An animal is one thing but this is disgusting." An association others had made and which added to its attraction. The head guard, sweating despite the cold, walked past, a padded cap held suggestively in his hand. In it rested the gleam of coins.

"What is it?" He shrugged at the question, pausing until a few coins had joined the others, smiling as he received his due. "Friends you are fortunate to have the privilege of seeing a product of the Chetame Laboratories. Note the coat, the eyes, the fangs. The body hair is as fine as fur, matted almost at the skin to form a natural armor. The hide itself is as tough as that of a bull. The fangs are copied from the stabbing teeth of a feline, while within the jaw lie the pointed molars of a carnivore."

He paused, waiting for the expected questions.

"The feet? They are modeled on those of a bird and can kick forward as well as back. The horns alone bear the touch of added artifice, as you can see by the gleam of metal tips. A worthy opponent for any hunter seeking a novel prey. A guardian of value for the protection of home and palace." He allowed himself to be humorous. "If any of you gentlemen wishes to safeguard the chastity of your woman then a beast such as this would be a good investment—but first make sure it has been gelded."

A titter followed the crude joke, one not appreciated by the woman who had spoken before.

"That's enough, Lou! If you want to stare at that thing then do it alone."

"Wait a few more minutes."

"No! I'm going! Come with me or don't bother to call again!"

The threat sent him to accompany her as she moved from the crowd. Others were not so squeamish. A guard yelled as a half-dozen young men, none robed, all a little intoxicated, thrust striped wands through the bars in an attempt to goad the beast.

"Are you mad? Back there! Back, damn you!"

"Fools!" The head guard glared his displeasure. "Have they nothing better to do?"

"Is it safe? Could it break loose?"

"No." The guard smiled as he reassured the man who'd asked. "But it's best not to torment the creature. Anger makes it hard to handle and we like to keep it quiet."

Nonetheless dilettantes laughed as they threw stones into the cage. Bored, jaded, the idle parasites of a struggling cul-

11

E. C. TUBB

ture, they considered themselves above the restrictions binding others. Dumarest heard the guard yell again as he moved away. Heard the mocking reply, the sudden snarl from the creature which filled the air with the raw taint of primeval fear, roar repeated as again the men goaded the beast.

The guards were fools. They bore clubs and should have used them. Instead they added to the din with futile shouting, a stupidity matched by the original error of displaying the creature in the first place.

The noise faded as he merged with the throng in the midway, listening to the siren call of a young girl offering a variety of exotic experiences: sensitapes which gave a full-sense illusion of reality; analogues which conveyed alternate pleasures; sexual coupling of beasts, killing, burning, dying, the terror of the chase, the thrill of the stalk; drugs to heighten perception, others to increase the sensitivity of nerves so that a touch became an ecstasy, a kiss unendurable pleasure; compounds to dull, to distort, to change; salves, pills, tablets, tonics—the girl offered them all.

"And you, my lord?" Her eyes met Dumarest's. "Is there nothing you desire?"

Nohing she could supply and she must have read the answer in his eyes. Oddly her own filled with tears.

"I am sorry, my lord," she whispered. "So very sorry."

A sensitive? It was possible, carnivals and fairs were natural resting places for such misfits. But what had she seen to make her cry? What had she guessed?

Perhaps nothing—the tears could have been a trick to attract others, a little showmanship to enhance her standing. A facile explanation, but Dumarest hesitated to accept it. A warning? It was possible and his back prickled to the familiar sense of danger. Podesta was the staging point for those heading for Ascelius. It was the cheap and easy way which was why it was popular with students and, at this time, it was simple to become lost in the crowd, which was why he had chosen to travel in the guise of a student. Had the girl seen through his pretense? Had she known that others had done so?

To pursue those questions would invite the very attention he needed to avoid. There was nothing he could do but to wait and remain inconspicuous.

He bought a skewer of meat from a stall and moved on

12

while he ate, pausing at the blaze of light thrown by lanterns over a gambling layout, watching as the dealer taught those placing bets how to manipulate the cards. A lesson they never even suspected—the man was good at his trade.

A crone offered vials of potion guaranteed to win adoration. A tall, gaunt man offered a drug which would increase the ability to memorize data. A woman with silver hair dotted with scarlet made crude jests as she persuaded a bunch of students to buy her system of mnemonics. A monk lifted a chipped bowl of worn plastic.

"Of your charity, brother."

Dumarest paused, tearing the last of the meat from the skewer and throwing aside the wood. The monk followed it with his eyes, saying nothing, but his meaning was plain. Dumarest had eaten—others would starve. If he could realize that, realize too that, but for the grace of God, he could be one of them, then the millennium would be that much closer. When all accepted the basic credo then it would have arrived.

Brother Lond would never see it. Mankind bred too fast, spread too quickly, but to cease from struggle because the aim was distant was alien to the Church of Universal Brotherhood of which he was a part.

Now he lifted his bowl, tall and gaunt in his robe of brown homespun, the bare feet in their sandals gnarled and stained with the dirt of the field, an old man who had dedicated his life to the easement of suffering. His head lowered as Dumarest dropped coins into the bowl.

"You are generous, brother."

Dumarest said dryly, "Aren't you going to wish me good fortune in my studies?"

"If it will please you." The sunken eyes of the monk were direct. "But do you go to study, brother? Or do you go to hide?"

A guess? Monks were far from being fools and the old man would have noticed his bearing, recognized the dun-colored robe for what it was, the charity as being alien to a student nursing his resources. A mistake, but not a serious one; Dumarest had no cause to fear the Church.

He moved on, halting to listen to a man selling electronic equipment.

"Small, neat and compact," he was saying. "Each unit is capable of multiple settings and can take a variety of programs. Use the earpiece while awake, the bone conductor when asleep—the actual emissions from the brain when the correct state is reached will trigger the instrument. Each cartridge holds an hour of continuous information, and a wide choice is available. Medicine, electronics, physics, astrogation—all in the form of lectures or assembled bits of essential data. Learn while you sleep. Gain the advantage of continuous study and ensure the gaining of your degree."

An honest man selling an honest product but a student wanted more than that. The vendor pursed his lips at the question.

"A crib? Something to take into the examination room and feed information as desired? My friend, if I had such an item I would be a criminal to sell it to you. The rooms are electronically guarded against such devices and, if you should be discovered owning one, you would be immediately expelled. I have no desire to contribute to another's ruin. I—" He broke off as a siren cut the air with its wail, a series of short and long blasts which ended in an echoing silence. "The *Cossos*." He looked at his audience. "That was her signal."

Dumarest's ship—it was time for him to board.

There was still a crowd clustered around the cage in its circle of brilliance, and as Dumarest passed he heard the raw, primitive snarl of the beast as it faced its tormentors. The guards, bribed, no longer made any effort to prevent the hail of missiles which the dilettantes threw at the cage, some hitting the bars, others the matted coat of the creature. They would tire of the sport or the beast would cease roaring its anger or its owner would come to complete the transshipment and the incident would be over and forgotten. But, perhaps, the taste would linger to remind humans that they were, at times, more viciously savage than any animal.

"Hurry!" A man called to his companion. "Let's get aboard before it's too late!"

There was no need to hurry; the warning signal had been a preliminary. It would be repeated later, again to warn of immediate departure. Even as Dumarest turned from the cage a siren blasted in the standard pattern and he halted, looking at the stubby shape which lifted from the dirt, the stained hull and patches vague beneath the blue shimmer of the Erhaft field which carried it up and out toward the stars.

The sight caught at the imagination, driving the beast insane.

Dumarest heard the sudden, maniacal scream of naked fury, the accompanying shrieks as the bars yielded and a guard died beneath the rake of sickle claws. Another joined him as the crowd raced from the spot, streaming like ants from the point of danger, jostling, thrusting, yammering their fear, their terror of the monster.

The beast stood roaring its hate and defiance, fists drumming on the barrel of its torso, saliva dripping from bared fangs, blood smeared on the claws, the matted hair.

"Lavinia! My God, Lavinia!"

The scream cut across the roaring, the drumming, the noise of the crowd. A sound torn from the throat of a woman in the extremity of anguish, shocking, desperate.

The thing heard it and dropped its hands, head turning to scan the area, seeing as Dumarest saw the small figure sprawled on the dirt, the mane of ebon hair, the glitter of the doll still clutched firmly in one hand.

"Lavinia!"

She didn't move, probably knocked unconscious from a blow delivered in unthinking panic, knocked down and half-stunned, dazed at least. Then the hand twitched, light catching the doll, flashing from the sequins, the tinsel, a sudden blaze of radiance which caught and held the attention of the beast, sent it padding toward the intriguing point of brightness, the nostrils flaring as it scented prey.

Things Dumarest noted as he moved, driving booted feet against the ground, the rush of wind filling his ears, catching at his hair. Wind which caught his robe and sent it to balloon behind him, a drag he fought to conquer.

Speed, to reach the small figure first, to distract the beast, to get her to safety. His eyes checked as he ran, assessing time and distance, seeing the tormented face of the girl's mother, Roy standing helplessly at her side, the small group of uniformed men behind them, faces pale blobs against the darkness of the running crowd.

Then he was stooping, scooping up the slight shape, lifting the girl to throw her high and far toward the reaching arms. He fell, shoulder and side numbed, to roll desperately from the foot which kicked at his face to miss and rip deeply into the dirt.

Lying, the taste of blood warm in his mouth, Dumarest looked at the death towering above him.

The beast was man-like but was not wholly a man. A true human would have killed without hesitation but the creature chose to roar, to snarl its hate and challenge—seconds which gave Dumarest his only chance.

He rolled again, climbing to his feet, backing to gain distance, the time to prepare. The blow which had knocked him down had ripped the robe into rags and he doffed the remnants to stand unhampered in neutral gray. A move and the knife lifted from his boot to fill his hand with edged and pointed steel. This was his only weapon, as the metal-mesh buried in the plastic of his clothing was his only defense. They and his body and brain were all he had. Together they had to be enough.

The beast snarled and darted forward, claws slashing the air as Dumarest jerked aside, feeling the grate of broken ribs, tasting again the saltiness of his own blood. A warning; to be too active was to rip a lung to shreds. Yet how to avoid the danger?

There was no safe way—the beast was too fast, too big and vicious. Backing, Dumarest studied it, searching for vulnerable points as he had before but now with more than casual interest. The throat, ridged and corded with muscle, would resist cuts and penetration. The genitals were buried deep between the massive thighs. The eyes were deep-set beneath prominent ridges of bone. The jaw was solid bone; the heart protected by the matted hair, the hide, the muscle and sinew beneath.

And the thing could kick forward as well as back, a thing Dumarest remembered as a foot ripped where he had been standing, talons naked, strong enough to disembowel. There was a moment in which the beast was off true balance and the knife rose, edge upwards, to catch the rear of the ankle, to bite, to cut as Dumarest dragged it free.

The beast roared, flailing the air, blood a ruby stream from the slashed joint. A small wound but one which hampered and made the thing a little less efficient.

It came forward again, snarling, relying on naked strength and size to crush and kill. Dumarest moved aside, dodged, moved again, conscious of the pain in his side, the blood in

16

his mouth. Blood he spat in a carmine stream as, ducking, the beast lunged.

For a moment the great head was lowered, the horns like two spears thrusting, to impale, to gore and rip and lift the screaming prey, to toss it high to be gored again as it fell. A demonstration of its weakness—the mistake its creators had made.

Dumarest spun, dodging the horns, conscious of the feet, feeling the slam as one hit the side of his thigh. His left hand fell to grip the beast's left horn, the lift of the head carrying him up as he threw his right leg over the back. As the thing reared he sent the point of his knife deep into an eye, twisting, thrusting, cursing as the width of the blade jammed against the orbital bone.

A moment wasted as he fought to free the steel then he was in the air, turning, twisting from the rake of the clawed hands which had swept him from his perch to hurl him far and hard against the dirt.

Roaring, the creature tore the knife from its eye and flung it after its attacker.

Dumarest watched it, saw the gleam of reflected light as it turned, the plume of dirt as it hit to skid to rest a score of yards from where he lay. To reach it would take time and yet without it he was helpless. To finish the job; to blind the creature so as to lock it in a cage of darkness while he left the range of its natural weapons—in that was his only safety.

He coughed and spat and ignored the blood, the pain which rasped his lungs with jagged glass. Beneath him the dirt quivered to the pound of feet as the beast rushed toward him, to kick and stamp until nothing was left, but a bloody smear. Dumarest rolled, scooped up a handful of dirt, threw it as he rose to fill the remaining eye with grit. He gained a moment as an inner lid cleansed the orb, and when next he rose the knife was again in his hand.

"Hold!"

He ignored the shout and the command, concentrating on the beast, the death rearing on clawed feet, turning now to spot him, the blood-smeared face a grotesque mask of bestial ferocity.

It would see him and attack, lowering the head to bring the horns into play as it had before. The trick was to stay on the

17

blind side, to avoid the lash of the foot, to send the point of the knife up and hard to ruin the remaining eye.

"Back, you fool! Back!"

Another shout, again ignored—the snarling creature demanded his entire attention. Dumarest sidled, facing the beast, tasting blood, feeling sweat dew his face, his palm, loosening his grip on the shaft of the knife; small things each of which could bring his end but there was no time to correct them now. He slowed, tempting the animal, showing himself, waiting, every nerve tense for the one, exact moment when he must move with smoothly oiled perfection.

Dirt rose beneath a scraping foot, furrows showing the rake of claws and, on the plated bone of the skull, a patch of reflected lavender moved, to glow again. to vanish as with a blur of movement the head lowered, horns lunging like twin spears as the massive thighs drove the thing at Dumarest.

He darted aside, felt agony tear at his lungs, saw the monstrous head turn vague as his sight became edged with darkness, felt the rasping impact of claws against hip and thigh as, almost too late, he spun to avoid the kick. Even as new pain joined the old, he was reaching, gripping, lifting the blade in a vicious, upward thrust at the far eye—knowing he had missed even as an arm swept around him to tighten, to crush him against the thick torso as, rising, the beast lifted him from his feet.

He dangled helpless, vomiting blood, staring at the blood-smeared mask above him, the jaws which gaped to show the dagger-like fangs, the pointed teeth. Jaws which lowered to his face, fangs which would rip the skin and flesh from the bone and leave nothing but a naked, grinning skull: the badge of the loser—the hallmark of death.

A moment, then he heard the dull and distant thuds, saw the sudden sprouting of feathered tubes in the thing's head and throat, felt the bruising sting as something drove into his neck—and fell into immediate and utter oblivion.

Chapter Two

He rose through layers of ebon chill counting seconds as he waited for the eddy currents to warm his body, for the pulmotor to cease aiding his respiration, for light and the euphoria of resurrection. A dream which dissolved into shattered fragments and the realization that he was not riding low, lying in a casket designed for the transportation of beasts, doped, frozen, ninety percent dead, risking the fifteen percent death rate for the sake of cheap travel.

A dream born of memory and followed by others; a surging tide of faces and places and strangely distorted images which threw him back into time in a series of speeded montages. Silver hair replaced by flaming scarlet, brown, gold ebon streaked with alabaster. A world on which the dead walked to converse with the living—a woman, a doll, a child—Lavinia!

He writhed as a tide of pain washed the images away and left him trembling but awake.

He looked up at a face. It was blurred, the planes and contours oddly vague as if seen through water or through eyes affected by chemical compounds. The face was haloed by the light beyond, rimmed with effulgence, touched with mystery.

Then, even as he looked, the features seemed to firm; the eyes widening to form limpid pools deep-set beneath arching brows, the nose firmly bridged, the cheeks concave, the rounded jaw strongly determined, the mouth wide, sensuous, the lips moist and full. The face was surmounted by a crested mane of hair which shone like oiled jet. An ebon cloud in which shone the sparkle of scintillate gems.

She said, "Earl Dumarest you are a fool."

"If so I am a grateful one, my lady. May I know my benefactor?"

"I am Charisse Chetame."

"Then, my lady, I thank you."

"For having saved your life?" Her laughter, like her voice, was deep and warm with resonance. "Please, Earl, don't compound your folly."

She could be playing a game with rules known only to herself if any such existed. Someone rich, jaded, choosing to amuse herself. One who could decide to terminate her charity—if charity it had been.

Dumarest struggled to sit upright, fighting a sudden nausea, taking deep breaths as he waited for it to pass. The bed was a hospital cot, the room fitted with medical equipment, his body naked beneath a thin sheet which fell as he rose to expose his torso, the scars which traced thin lines over his chest. In the hollows of his elbows small wounds rested puckered mouths in tiny gardens of bruise.

"Intravenous feeding," she explained, unnecessarily. "You've been under slowtime. Six weeks subjective."

Over a normal day he had lain, his metabolism speeded by the drug, healing with accelerated tempo. Even though he'd been fed, his body showed signs of wastage.

"You were cut up pretty badly inside," she explained casually. "I had to section the bone and replace quite a large amount of lung tissue. I didn't think you'd object to a couple more scars." Her hand lifted, a slender finger touching his skin, tracing a path over the pattern of cicatrices. A touch which held more than a professional interest, lingering as if a caress. "A fighter," she mused. "You've worked in the ring and learned the hard way. How often have you killed Earl?"

Too often, but he said nothing, watching her eyes, the set of her lips. She was past her first youth, in her third decade at least, and the name was familiar. Chetame? He remembered the guard.

He said. "The beast was yours?"

"Is, Earl. It's still alive and the sight has been fully restored. You know what happened, of course?" She didn't wait for him to reply. "My men had to shoot it with anesthetic darts. One of them hit you. They brought you in together."

And who had claimed her first attention?

"It was deliberate," he said, understanding. "You placed the creature outside to be tormented. Only a fool would have done such a thing without reason and, my lady, I do not take you for a fool."

"Charisse, Earl, you may call me Charisse. And you are correct. It was necessary for me to discover its tolerance level and also its potential strength. Clients do not take kindly to being supplied with beasts they cannot control. The cage seemed strong enough but, obviously, it was not. And I had underestimated the maniacal fury level by a factor of at least five percent. It could even be ten."

A mistake—and two guards had died and the child could have joined them. The men standing by had been slow to act or had been ordered to hold their fire. More tests?

"That's why I called you a fool, Earl." Charisse seemed oblivious to Dumarest's anger. "To have risked your life for so little. A child. Something so easily replaced. But perhaps you had a personal reason?"

She guessed too much and Dumarest remembered the montage of dreams; the images, names, faces which had spun before him. Had he raved in delirium? Talked in answer to direct questions? She knew his name which was a clue in itself. How deeply had she probed?

She stepped back as he threw his legs over the edge of the cot to stand upright, the sheet wrapped around his waist. A tall woman, deep-breasted, her hips and buttocks a harmony of curves. The outline of her thighs showed taut against the embroidered fabric of her gown. She emitted a delicate perfume: a blend of rose and carnation coupled with a scent he did not recognize, but which made him acutely aware of her femininity.

She said, "You need to take things easy for a while. Good

food and rest and no undue exertion. Your system has been shocked in more ways than one."

"I have to go somewhere."

"I know. To Ascelius." She shrugged at his expression. "It's obvious. You wore a student's robe and where else do ships head for at this time? Which was yours? The *Evidia*? The *Qualt*?"

"The *Cossos*."

"You blame me for having missed it?"

He said flatly, "The beast was yours. You failed to contain it. If it hadn't broken free I'd be on my way by now."

"Are you forgetting I saved your life?"

"No. And, once again, I thank you."

"Thank me?" She shook her head. "What value are words? You know better than to think payment can be made by a babble of gratitude. Tell me, Earl, of what value is life? If you were dying now, at this moment, and I had the drug which could save you—how much would you be willing to pay?"

Without hesitation he said, "All I possess. Of what value are goods without life to enjoy them?"

"A true philosopher." Her smile was radiant. "Earl, you are a man after my own heart. But enough of this silly bickering. There need be no debts between us and certainly no animosity. Shall we drink to it?"

"Like this?"

"What?"

She hadn't grasped his meaning. Patiently he explained. "My lady—Charisse—I have no clothes."

They had been refurbished; the gray plastic smooth, bearing a rich sheen, the protective mesh hidden from sight. The knife too had been polished and honed and Dumarest lifted it from where it lay on the plate and noted the thin line of unbroken weld beneath the pommel before slipping it into his boot.

From where she stood pouring wine Charisse said, "A vicious blade, Earl. But you know how to use it." As she handed him a goblet filled with sparkling amber liquid she added, "No other man would have survived ten seconds after the mannek had reached him."

"I was lucky."

"And fast." Her lips touched the goblet, wine adding to their moistness. "So very fast. I've never seen a man with such reflexes. We must talk about it but, first, we drink and then we dine. To you, Earl, and a fortunate meeting."

"To you, Charisse," he responded. "And to your loveliness."

He hadn't intended the words but they came easily to his lips, as did others when they had sat to share dishes of pounded meats and vegetables, compotes of fruit and honey, an assortment of oddly shaped biscuits, morsels of varying tastes and textures. The meal was served by a soft-footed girl with a blank, unformed face, a slight creature who served and bowed and left at a signal.

"An idiot," said Charisse casually as if expecting Dumarest to ask the question. "I've done what I could but the basic gene structure was rotten to begin with."

"A local?"

"No." She took a sip of wine, lavender this time, tart with citrus. "Podestanians aren't to be trusted."

Which was why they stayed in her vessel? Dumarest itched to examine it but knew better than to insist. As a guest he had to defer to his hostess but he wondered what the ship could contain, how the holds had been designed.

"You're curious, Earl." She met his eyes. "Don't bother to deny it. Who am I? What am I doing? What do I intend? Questions easily answered. I own the Chetame Laboratories. I deal in manufactured life forms and will supply any who have the price to buy. Gene manipulation, forced growth, breeding for desired characteristics—you must know the kind of thing. Know too why you interest me so much. Your speed and determination are unusual traits and should be cultivated. You would be surprised to learn how many women yearn for the perfect mate to provide perfect offspring. How many would be willing to pay highly for selected sperm with a guarantee as to results and quality. Not to speak of the men who want strong and prideful sons. More wine?"

She poured without waiting for an answer, leaning close across the table so as to fill his nostrils with the scent of her perfume. She radiated an almost feral heat, stirred his masculinity, smiled as, sitting back, she held him with her eyes.

"My father taught me most of what I know," she said. "He died last year and the laboratories came to me. My mother was a geneticist trained on Shaldom—they are far advanced in the art of chromosome unification. A man with two heads, a woman with four arms—pay for it and they will supply it."

"And you?"

"Freaks and distortions don't interest me. The mannek was developed from a basic human sperm with additions to form a near invulnerable form of life which—"

"Proved a failure."

"—could. . . . What did you say?"

"The thing is a failure." Dumarest elaborated as he sipped at his wine. "You made another mistake, Charisse. The multiplication of attributes does not result in added efficiency."

He had touched her as he'd intended and he watched her react to the slight on her ability; the clenching of her hands, the tension of her jaw, the bunching of small facial muscles which, somehow, made her look old. The moment passed as she shielded her face behind her goblet, throat working as she drank wine.

"The horns," he explained as she lowered the near empty container. "The claws. The feet, the jaws. Some animals have a double attack system—a cat, for example, with its claws and teeth. Some use head and feet, like a bird with its beak and talons. A bull has its horns."

"So?"

"Those systems have been designed by trial and error over thousands of years. Add them and you show flaws. To use the horns the mannek has to stoop. Once it does that it loses a degree of vision. To kick and gore at the same time is to diversify effort. To rend with the claws is to ignore the horns. To—need I go on?"

She said bluntly, "Could you have killed it?"

"No."

"Not even if you'd had your full strength? If you hadn't been hurt at the outset?" She added, "Using your knife, naturally."

He said, "You know the answer to that. The natural defenses are too high. To stab and slash takes time and the wounds would be relatively minor."

"But if your life depended on it?"

He would do his best but too much could happen; a slip, the flick of blood into his eyes, sweat easing his grip, the rake of a claw, the shift of the wind, the glare of reflected sunlight. Never could he be certain of winning. No man could ever be that.

"Earl?"

She was insistent and he wondered why. Wondered too what she could have learned while he was being treated. While under slowtime nothing could have been gained but at the end, or if he had been returned to normal time for a few hours, he would have been vulnerable. Drugs, hypnotism, electronic probing. He remembered the dreams, the stimulated memories, the result of distorted senses. The result of applied instruction? And why the terminal wave of pain?

She shrugged when he asked. "A means to restore full awareness. It was created by direct cortical stimulation and caused no cellular damage. Now, Earl, please answer my question."

"I can't." He was bluntly honest. "How the hell can I? You're asking me to predict a certainty and only God can do that."

"Or the Cyclan?" She smiled as he made no answer. "We're bickering again, Earl, and without need. Like young lovers so tensed with emotion they explode at a word. It's my fault. I should have remembered you have just awakened from treatment. But think of it, Earl. You matched against a mannek. The odds against your winning would be astronomical. With skilled management you could make a fortune."

The glittering prospect had lured too many to their death and he wondered why she had mentioned it. And why mention the Cyclan? Coincidence, perhaps, but Dumarest distrusted coincidences and had long learned the error of taking things at their apparent value. The woman could be what she claimed or she could be that and more.

She looked up as he rose, the clean lines of her throat a column of perfection, the gems in her hair winking, moving, sparkling, drifting among the ebon tresses like a host of watching eyes. Tiny orbs held his own as she too rose, to step toward him, to fill his nostrils with her scent before stepping to where a mass of cut and shaped crystal stood in an elaborate form on a small table to one side of the salon.

"A toy, Earl, let me show it to you."

"Thank you, Charisse, but I haven't the time. I've things to do, a passage to arrange, you understand."

"Of course." She disarmed him with her agreement. "But there are no ships just yet. In a few days the *Ophir* is due and the *Kevore* shortly afterward. They come to pick up any remaining students. You could book passage on either."

"And you?"

"I'm waiting to transship the mannek. After that I return to the laboratories on Kuldip." She lifted a hand toward the crystal. "Now let me show you my toy."

It came alive beneath her hand, light winking, fading to flare again in a kaleidoscope of shifting points, burning, transient brilliance, accompanied by a musical chiming, a brittle tintinnabulation which filled the chamber and echoed to ring again in new and more complex patterns. Light and sound. Brilliance and tinklings. Form and movement and a vague disquiet.

The unease was quashed as Charisse came to him to throw back her head and smile into his eyes with her hair alive with scintillations.

Dumarest smelled her perfume. Felt the blood pound in his veins. Felt the age-old urge dictated by nature—the force designed to perpetuate the species. Tasted blood as his teeth dug into the soft inner flesh of his cheek.

"Here, Earl." Her voice was soft as she handed him more wine. Bubbles rose in glowing emerald to burst, to be renewed, to die in eye-catching sparkles. "Drink it, my darling. It will do you good. Give you strength and help you to relax." Then, as he hesitated, "You almost died, Earl. You would have died had it not been for me. Trust me, my darling. Drink the wine. Drink."

Drink and add to the drugs already circulating in his system. The compounds which could have been added to the nutrients fed into his veins. Yet to be cautious now was to be wary too late. If this were a trap he was snared. If it were to be sprung he had no escape. Her guards, while unseen, would be close.

"Earl?" She was insistent. "Drink, Earl. Drink!"

Light and music. Shine and glitter and the sweet, brittle tinkling of endlessly ringing crystal. The perfume assailed his senses and turned his yearning into an impatient fire.

Pheremones, chemical messengers emitted by her glands to trigger his masculine response. An aphrodisiac against which there was no defense. A demand impossible for him to resist.

"You want me, my darling," she whispered. "You burn with need. Hold me, Earl. Hold me!"

Hold and feel the warmth, the softness and comfort which came from the union of parts, the completeness, the merging. To yield to the prime dictate built into the basic fabric of his being; the survival urge which overrode all else.

To mate. To die while mating—but to mate! The compulsion to procreate in which the individual was nothing more than the carrier of the precious and selfish genes; seed to be sown in a blaze of physical heat and a desire which rose to a crescendo, obliterating all caution, all restraint. A need which turned Dumarest into a rutting beast rewarding him with the intoxication of ecstasy.

In a small room which had once known exotic delights Cyber Okos experienced an intoxication of a different kind. It was always the same after rapport had been broken with the massed brains of central intelligence and the engrafted Homochon elements within his skull sank back into normal quiescence. A time in which the machinery of his body began to realign itself with mental control while he drifted in a dark void sensing strange memories and new concepts, scraps of data, novel outlooks. The overflow from other, distant intelligences. Intriguing glimpses of other worlds which he would never see but which were as real as any he had known.

A familiar experience—Okos had long been a servant of the Cyclan, but this time there had been something new.

Lying supine he thought about it. A fragment which had become implanted on his brain during the moment when central intelligence had assimilated his data as if it had been water sucked by a sponge. Near instantaneous communication against which the speed of light was a crawl gave the Cyclan a part of the power it possessed. Data given and instructions received—but this time there had been that little extra.

A mistake? The concept alone was disturbing for central intelligence was above such mundane error or it was no better than a flawed machine. Deliberate, then, but why? Why should he have been selected to be given that fragment of data?

This was an illogical thought and immediately he corrected the error. He had no proof that others had not been given the

27

information and yet the probability against it was, had to be, in the order of ninety-nine percent—a prediction as close to absolute certainty as he dared to make. So, working on the assumption that he had been favored, the question remained.

Why?

Opening his eyes, Okos stared up at the reflection in the mirrored ceiling. Lying on the bed he looked a corpse dressed in the scarlet of his robe, the shaven head framed by the cowl, gaunt, smooth, skull-like, only the deep-set eyes revealing life and intelligence. A man dedicated to an organization whose seal was blazoned on the breast of the garment he wore. A living, breathing, emotionless machine. One with the ability to take a handful of facts and from them extrapolate a whole. Of taking a situation and predicting the logical outcome of any course of action. Now, looking at his reflection, he assessed what he had just learned.

Some of the associated brains which formed central intelligence had shown signs of aberration.

Elge, the Cyber Prime, would never have released this information, and to Okos it was plain why. Once hint at the possibility of incipient madness and the one great reward every cyber worked to obtain, the assimilation of his brain at the end of his working life into the giant complex, would lose its appeal. And what could replace it?

For some, Okos among them, the work itself was enough—the striving to replace error with reasoned calculation, to eliminate the vagaries of emotional dictates with the cold logic of assessed benefit. To spread the domination of the Cyclan until it embraced every world in the known galaxy. An end desired by all who wore the scarlet robe, augmented by the conviction that, even after physical termination, the intelligence would live on in the brain which, removed from the body, would rest in a vat filled with nutrients, kept alive and aware by the magic of science, locked in series with the others which had gone before to become a part of the gestalt of central intelligence.

But, if some of the brains had gone insane?

Okos rose, touching the wide band of golden metal at his left wrist, ending the zone of silence which had added to the security of locked and guarded doors. A precaution against electronic spies while he had been in communication with the heart of the Cyclan. As he opened the door an acolyte bowed in respectful deference; a young man dedicated to serve his master, still in training, one who need never gain the coveted distinction Okos had achieved.

"Master?"

"Have Chan and Elcar check all ship movements and arrivals during the past two days. Send word to Corcyn for data on the Fenilman Project. Gather all agents' reports and have them on my desk in an hour."

"All, master?" Ashir looked doubtful. "The mass of data is great and much must be valueless."

This attitude would keep him a acolyte and would cost him dear if maintained. No data was ever without value. Each small fact, trifling as it might appear, could provide the essential key to unlock a puzzle, provide the answer to an apparently insoluble problem.

"Obey." Okos did not raise his voice and the smooth modulation of his tone remained unaltered but the acolyte bowed and seemed to cringe a little. "Do any wait?"

"Two, master. The manager of the Vard Federation and Professor Pell of the Paraphysical Laboratory of the Higham University."

Men who wanted the services the Cyclan offered and Okos would see them both—there would be time while the data was assembled, and the business of the Cyclan never hesitated.

"Show in the manager. His name?"

"Mahill Shad."

He was round, plump, sweating a little and radiating anxiety. A typical product of a culture which thought that to consume was to progress. He came directly to the point.

"I am here on business, Cyber Okos, and it's possible you could help me. I will, naturally, pay for any advice you see fit to give."

"Is that all you want? Advice?"

"Well—" Shad hesitated, suddenly conscious of his crudity, suddenly aware of what the tall, calm man at the desk represented. Cybers were not hired as common workmen and not all could gain their services. To forget the power of their organization was to invite disaster in more ways than one. He tried again. "I've come to Ascelius to recruit graduates for our interests on Lemos; we have an extensive mining project there with associated developments in bacteriological culture farms. The problem is how many to hire for how long and in just what fields. Our computer has provided an analogue, of course, but—" The spread of his hands completed the sentence. A computer was only as good as the data it contained, the operators in charge, the programmers who made up the schedules. "A form of insurance," he ended. "A mistake could be costly in contract terms, voidances and compensation for work shifts."

"I understand." Okos knew more than the other guessed but said nothing. The mines on Lemos would run into trouble in a matter of months when the shafts hit a strata of geological instability. The bacteriological farms would be faced with competition from a new process already proved on a nearby planet. Men hired now would be a liability. "I will forward your request for the services of the Cyclan," he said smoothly. "If you are accepted and the fees can be agreed then the matter can be resolved."

"But—" Shad was impatient. "Can't you give me the answer now?"

"No. Leave details of how you can be contacted." Then, as the man still hesitated, Okos added, "Or am I to understand you are no longer interested?"

A hint taken as the veiled threat it was and Shad left, protesting his interest. Impatience would drive him to hire the men and time would ruin him. The Vard Federation, driven desperate, would beg the help of the Cyclan which would be provided at a price. The advice, followed, would be of value and a foothold would have been gained in the company and on its world. A foothold was all the Cyclan needed. Once established the organization would be in demand and in a matter of years would be the true power behind the façade.

Professor Pell had a different problem.

"It's a matter of academic values," he said as he plumped into a chair. "The Higham University is in the process of reorganization and my department is regarded as of small value. I wondered if—that is—well . . ."

He was begging but connected to the scholastic establishment and of potential use.

Okos said, "The paraphysical sciences have recently gained an impetus from the discoveries of Doctor Ahmed Rafiq of the University of Zabouch. His report on a hundred sensitives tested under stringent laboratory conditions is a telling document. I could get you a copy."

"Would you?" Pell had succeeded beyond his wildest hopes. "If you could I would be grateful. If at any time I could serve you please ask." He left, protesting his gratitude, not guessing that he would be asked to pay and, having paid, would continue to do so.

The Cyclan always had a use for agents.

Alone Okos studied the data Ashir had provided. A mass of items which the cyber checked, valued, assessed, assimilated, fed into the computer which was his brain. Facts to build a pattern. Data to forge a trap for a man.

Dumarest had been on Elysius, that was a fact established beyond all doubt. He had left on the *Mercador*. The ship had touched on several worlds on a regular schedule—on which had Dumarest left it? To which had he gone?

Okos had narrowed the choice down to two, working on a basis of pure logic adapted to local conditions and associated factors. If Dumarest was aware that he was being hunted, and the probability of that was in the order of ninety-three percent, then his actions would be influenced by that knowledge. The region was one of poor worlds with limited economies among which a ship would need to work hard to earn a profit. For such ships the exodus of scholars from Podesta would provide a welcome source of revenue. And how better to hide than among a crowd?

On the other hand, guessing that he was being searched for, knowing the power of the Cyclan he could have made for Quen there to wait for the hunting season to open and the tourists to arrive with the increase in shipping such trade would entail.

Two probabilities—which was correct?

The communicator came to life beneath his touch.

"Ashir—bring me the latest data received from the worlds of Podesta and Quen."

On the latter there had been rape, murder, theft, a ship delayed for no apparent reason, an accident in which a waiting hunter had blown off his foot, the second-hand report of a man who had wronged another and had died beneath the thrust of a knife. A second and Okos passed on; the victim had been a gambler, the killer a man who had lost too much. A clue, perhaps, but the probability was low.

31

On Podesta a man had rescued a child.

Okos checked the region, the details, absorbing the data at a glance and feeling the glow of mental satisfaction at having made a correct prediction which was the only pleasure he could know. Podesta—Dumarest had revealed himself—revealed too the world which must be his destination.

A window filled one wall of the room and Okos turned toward it, halting to stare through the crystal at the mass of buildings beyond—the spires and towers, domes and turrets, parapets and peaks all adorned with variegated flags denoting different universities, various seats of learning, the clustered departments, the massed halls. The product of a world whose main industry was the imparting of knowledge and which sprawled in city-sized confusion.

Even as he watched another ship settled on the distant field to discharge its cargo of fresh students. Another batch to add to the hordes which thronged the streets and lodging houses, the eating places and taverns, the emporiums, the bookstores, the cut-price tutorials. A mass of variegated humanity, nondescript in their ubiquitous robes. Soon Dumarest would be among them—when would he arrive?

Chapter Three

It had rained, the downpour followed by freezing winds which had turned the water into ice, coating the buildings with a glistening frost which glittered in the late afternoon sun as if the towers and spires and soaring peaks had been dusted with crushed and scattered jewels. Against the white brilliance the flags displayed their varied hues, their markings, their shapes: oblong, square, forked, lozenged, some with puffs and slashes, others with a stark and simple dignity.

"Damn!" The man at Dumarest's side stamped his feet, white plumes of vapor wreathing his uplifted cowl. "I hate the cold!"

Rani Papandrious, a merchant and a successful one, now aimed to acquire a degree and the entry it would give him to the higher echelons of society on his home world. Beyond him a girl sucked in her breath as she stared with wide eyes at the flags, the frosted buildings. She had been backed by her family and launched into a strange environment in a desperate hope that she would provide for them all.

Papandrious shook his head as she walked from the field toward a group of waiting figures.

"They'll skin her," he said with professional cynicism.

33

"Take all she's got and then leave her stuck in a slum dormitory, classes she can't handle, a job she won't be able to keep."

A judgment Dumarest didn't share. Those waiting were students with little love for the hovering vultures and, while they might sponge on the girl's generosity, they would be fair in their fashion. She would pay but she would learn and, later, she too could be meeting the new arrivals.

As could Bard Holman who had been the last down the ramp after arguing with the captain. A dispute he was reluctant to abandon.

"We have a case," he complained. "Passage booked to Ascelius and nothing said about diversions and pickups and delays on the way. I've lost classes and time and both will cost money. An extra semester will ruin my budget. The way I see it we're all entitled to a compensatory payment."

A fledgling lawyer, city-bred, inexperienced in the ways of space, he had no case. The captain had provided what he had contracted to supply and had probably lost money on the deal.

Sheen Agostino smiled as he stamped away. She was small and round and dark and had come to gain a post-graduate degree in computer programming, a woman with an innocent openness gifted with the ability to recognize the humor of every situation.

"So young," she said. "And so impatient. So eager to learn and to conquer his world. Even to listen to him makes me feel old."

Papandrious was gallant. "You don't look it, Sheen. In fact you look really lovely. You agree, Earl?"

"Of course."

"What else could a gentleman say?" Her tone held laughter but her eyes were grateful. "Well, friends, I guess it's time for us to part."

"But we'll meet again?" The merchant was eager to establish a comfortable relationship. "I'll contact you," he promised. "In a couple of days after we've settled down. We can have a meal, and talk, and share mutual entertainment." Courtesy made him turn to Dumarest. "And you, Earl? You will join us?"

"Thank you, but no." Dumarest saw the relief in the man's eyes. "I'll be too busy. I've a lot of catching up to do."

"You will, Earl." Sheen was positive. "And you'll make the best geologist this world has ever produced. Just keep thinking that."

This was basic advice to bolster a determination which could falter when faced with harsh reality, but even as she gave it she recognized how little he needed it. A recognition which made her feel a little stupid.

Dumarest came to her rescue, building on the lie he had told, the story he had given his fellow passengers to assuage their curiosity.

"I'll remember that, Sheen, and when I feel like quitting it'll help. It's just that I could have waited too long. Maybe, with the best instructors, well, we'll see."

A seed sown for future reaping if the need should arise. Her studies would give her access to the computers with their stored data, but to ask too much too soon would be to invite rejection or, worse, a sharpened curiosity. Later, if necessary, he would contact her and she would remember his present indecision.

Now she said, "Just don't rush into anything, Earl. Take your time and study the prospects. You'll find a complete listing of all available courses together with fees, times and such at any of the information booths. The ones operated by the combined universities can be trusted to deliver what they promise. The free-lance establishments may promise a short-cut and cheap tutorials but you need to be a genius to gain from their offers." She held out a hand, slender fingers touching his own, before falling back to her side. "Good luck, Earl."

Luck had saved him often in the past and he needed it now more than ever. Standing alone before the bulk of the vessel he looked over the field. To one side the wind caught a scatter of debris and lifted it to send it swirling in a drifting cloud of fragments which dissolved to fall in a powdery rain. Biodegradable material falling into their basic constituent elements beneath the action of sunlight and temperature change.

A good sign—Ascelius promised to be a clean world.

The shadows were lengthening when Dumarest left the field. The group of loungers had mostly dispersed, those remaining despite the growing cold ignoring him as he passed, sensing their attentions would be unwanted, their interest unwelcome. He ignored them in turn; the answers he needed

35

would come from those less fortuitously placed. Ascelius might be clean but it was still a jungle and a dun-colored robe could mask a predator more dangerous than any beast.

He walked on, deeper into the city, heading for the busy streets and areas, watching for those who followed for too long and too close, those who stared too hard, those who looked away too soon. Small signs which could betray those with a special interest. He saw none and entered a tavern when lights began to glow from lamps fixed high on the walls. It was as he'd expected, a room set with tables and benches, a bar at one end, a counter bearing dishes of various foods presided over by a stout man with a shock of gray hair and a face seamed with time.

"Fill your plate for a vell, stranger." His voice was a boom. "Bread an extra five mins." He watched as Dumarest made his selection. "Just arrived?"

"It shows?"

"To an experienced eye." The man nodded at the plate which could have held more. "The longer you stay the hungrier you get. Not many students come in here who don't pile their plate as high as it will go. You want wine?" He beamed at Dumarest's nod. "Take a seat and the girl will serve you." His voice rose to a roar. "Trisha!"

She was tall, thin, her face bearing a waxen pallor, the eyes sunk in circles of darkness. Her hair, blonde, hung in a lank tangle. Beneath the rough gown she wore her figure was shapeless. The hands which tilted the flagon over Dumarest's goblet were little more than flesh stretched over bone.

A student, he guessed, working to pay for her tuition, starving herself to pay her fees. She watched as he paid for the wine, added five mins as a tip. As she reached for the coins he dropped a two-vell piece before her hand.

"For you, Trisha." He noted the hesitation, the inner struggle, and added, quickly, "For nothing but your time. Sit and share wine with me. It's allowed?"

"If there's profit in it then it's allowed." She poured a second goblet, watched as Dumarest paid for it, took a cautious sip. "Do I have to drink it?"

"No. I just want to talk."

She said softly, "You could be wasting your time. If you hope to buy me forget it. I'm not that desperate."

"I need a little help," said Dumarest. "I want to save time and fees—there is a charge made for information?"

"You name it and there's a charge." She sipped more wine, relaxing. "What do you want to know?" She listened then looked across the chamber. "Lahee's your man. I'll send him over."

Like the girl he was tall, thin, bearing the same marks of emaciation. He sat and picked up the wine she had left, throwing back his head as he drank without invitation. An accepted member of the fraternity, his robe stained, the capacious pockets bulging, the array of flags and pennants stitched to his breast frayed and faded. A friend, he had been given the chance to win what he could.

"Trisha tells me you want to learn things. Save money at the booths. Maybe I can help."

"If you can't then send me someone who can," said Dumarest. "And pay for that wine before you go."

"It was Trisha's!"

"You want to argue about it?" Dumarest held the other's eyes, spoke more gently as they dropped from his own. "I can guess the system—pass me along for as long as the traffic will bear, right? Well, the chain ends here. You know what I want, can you supply it?"

"Geology," said Lahee. "You want to know all about rocks." He dug into his pockets and produced papers, books, a pen with which he made rapid notations in a neat and precise script. "If you've the money to pay for it the Puden University is the best. Try and get with Etienne Emil Fabull. If he's booked solid you could bribe someone to yield his place. I'll handle it for you if you like." He paused, hopefully, sighed as Dumarest made no answer. "Well, let's run over the other prospects."

He droned on, listing various colleges and instructors, balancing their relative values, touching on the scale of fees and other expenses. Dumarest listened to the list with apparent interest while he studied the speaker. Lahee was older than he had seemed at first; much of the emaciated appearance stemmed from the passage of time as well as from the lack of food. A perpetual student, he had found a niche in this academic jungle and made it his way of life. An accredited student still, but now more a parasite than an eager seeker after knowledge.

37

But safer to use than a computer.

They could be monitored, fitted with response triggers to check anyone asking a certain type of question or adjusted to file the details of all making inquiries. That risk he preferred to avoid.

As Lahee fell silent Dumarest said, "Thank you. You've been most helpful and I appreciate it."

"Glad to hear it." The man moved the scatter of books and papers before him, gathering them into a neat pile, the sheet he had marked close to one hand. "Would you say half the booth fee was fair?"

"It seems reasonable." Dumarest looked at the books, noting their age and condition. The covers were frayed, the spines cracked and gaping, pages obviously loose—rarities here on Ascelius where there was a vested interest in the elimination of old textbooks and manuals. Undegraded only because of their owners' care. "May I?" He reached for them before Lahee could object. "If you're hungry eat," he suggested. The food he'd bought was still untouched on his plate. "A bonus."

"You'll be careful?" Lahee was anxious despite the hunger which drove him to the food. "Those things are my living."

"I'll be careful."

Dumarest gently turned the pages. Only one book held anything of real interest, but he scanned it as casually as he had the rest. A list of names, subjects and the colleges at which they had been associated dating from some fifteen years earlier to four years from the present. Most of those listed would still be teaching, some could be dead, one in particular certainly was.

Dumarest looked at the name, the college at which the man had taught, one of the answers he had come to find.

Clyne was old, matched only by Higham, beaten only by Schreir. An equal partner in the Tripart which formed the acme of scholastic renown on Ascelius. The original building had long since been overlaid by massive extensions; the rooms, dormitories, laboratories and halls spreading and rearing to form towering pinnacles surmounted by the proudly arrogant flags of emerald blazoned with a scarlet flame. A throbbing hive of industry with teeming students studying as they slept and as they ate on a rigid, three shifts a day schedule. A machine designed to instill knowledge and to set the stamp of achievement with acknowledged degrees.

At times Myra Favre thought of it as a thing alive; the data-stuffed computers the brain, the atomic power plant the heart, the students and faculty the corpuscles flowing through the arteries of corridors, the pulsing nodes of chambers. An analogy born from her early study of medicine before she had realized her lack of suitability for the field, just as she had later learned that physics was not for her, nor geology, nor astronomy. She had wasted years before she had found her niche in administration and friends and good fortune had established her in her present position.

"Myra?" Heim Altman smiled from the screen of her communicator. "Just an informal word. Convenient?"

A shake of the head and he would break the connection to wait for her return call. Returning his smile she said, "Go ahead."

"Just thought we could discuss a few things. How are you on available space?"

"Short as always. Why do you ask?"

"I've an idea which could expand your potential. Registrations are low on some of our non-industrial subjects and I thought we could arrange a mutually beneficial exchange. Higher number takes over the smaller. Agreed?"

"In principle, yes." She maintained her smile. "You know I'm always willing to cooperate, Heim. Why don't you send over a list of classes and numbers and I'll run a comparison check before making a final decision. Of course you won't send me any deadbeats and debtors, will you?"

"Only honest to God paid-up students, Myra. You know you can trust me."

As she could trust a predator, she thought as the screen went dead, her smile dying with the image. Altman would unload all the rubbish he could, and she would do the same to him if given the chance—classes which had proved to be failures, instructors not worth their salt, students who hovered on the edge of debt. Always it was the same after a new intake and always there were problems which had to be solved one way or another. A part of her job was to solve them. Another was to insure the financial profitability of the university. Fail on either and Clyne would have a vacancy for someone to fill her place.

39

"Madam Favre?" Her secretary appeared, a young, well-made girl with a thick tress of golden hair draped over one shoulder. "You asked for a report on the latest enrollments."

"Bring it in."

The resumé was as she had expected—high enrollments in the usual courses, less on the non-industrial, a few hopeless subjects which must be pruned or compromises made. Pursing her lips she studied the details. Professor Koko would have to face reality or subsidize his classes from his own pocket, and knowing the man, she could guess at the reaction her ultimatum would bring. Another argument she could do without and there would be more if she agreed to Altman's suggestion and switched students from Clyne to Schrier. Yet the books had to be balanced and no dead weight could be tolerated.

Had she failed?

The fear was always present and each time after a new intake came the moment of truth. If student enrollment was low in certain subjects then she was wrong to have agreed they should be included in the curriculum. If tutors proved unpopular, the same. Too many mistakes and she would have demonstrated her failure to make valid judgments. One too many and her career would be in ruins. And she was too old to start again.

Unconsciously her hands rose to her face, fingers searching for the telltale signs of flaccidity she knew must soon become obvious. As yet she looked as she had ten years ago but the years were passing and each worked its measure of destruction. In another ten years visitors would cease to regard her as a woman almost too young to hold her responsible position. In another twenty they might regard her as too old.

"Madam?" The secretary again and Myra almost snapped her irritation before she remembered to smile. The girl meant well and it wasn't her fault that she owned such an attractive face and figure. Not her fault that she was young. "Doctor Boyce asks you to call."

"Make the connection." Myra waited, fuming at the ridiculous protocol which demanded that she, the inferior, contact the Dean, the superior, even though his secretary had made the initial contact. Why the hell couldn't he have just rung direct? She arranged her face as he looked from the screen,

40

her smile a blend of pleasure and deference. "Dean! This is a pleasure!"

His smile was as mechanical as her own. "One shared, Myra. We don't talk often enough but you know how it is. At times I wish we could find some method of extending the day. To be brief I've been checking the enrollments and I'm not too happy. You have the matter in hand, of course?"

"Of course, Dean." Inwardly she wondered who had been carrying tales. The secretary? It was possible—that baby smile could mask a scheming brain. "It is merely a matter of simple adjustment. In a few days, I assure you, the stockholders will have no possible grounds for complaint."

She saw by his expression she had hit the target, but he was quick to refute such mundane considerations. "My concern is for the academic side, Myra. The standards of Clyne must be maintained. We want no stupid nonsense such as other establishments indulge in simply to attract large enrollments. Reuben, for example, with their one-semester guaranteed-degree course in anatomical manipulation. Or Professor Pell who—" He broke off, remembering, fearful of saying too much. Higham was of the Tripart and Pell taught in Higham. "I won't go into detail, my dear, but you can appreciate my concern. I just thought I'd let you know the atmosphere, so to speak."

"Thank you, Dean."

She was still being formal despite his attempt to get on a more friendly footing and he was old and wise enough in his craft to sense that he could have pressed too hard too soon, yielded too quickly to the promptings of those who had no interest in the university but the profits it brought them.

"I knew you'd understand, my dear." His smile was one of fatherly concern. "The pressure of work—how well I know it! Perhaps you should take a short rest. A few days away from the grind if you can manage it. Sometimes a break enables one to obtain a fresh point of view."

"Yes," she agreed. "I guess you're right. Thank you for the advice." Her smile told him all was forgiven. "And thank you, Kevork, for your concern and interest."

He could shove that right where it would hurt the most, she thought as the screen died. The interfering old bastard! Had it been her secretary? Cleo was ambitious but had she the ability to be so guileful? Had it been Jussara of Higham?

A possibility, the bitch was jealous and had made a bad mistake giving Pell the go-ahead. Or was it simply someone hungry for her position, in which case the field was too wide to investigate.

Again she studied the resumé, finding the facts and figures as depressing as before. The profit was there—the usual courses insured that, but to the stockholders each tutor and every inch of space should show a return. Greed, she thought, the prime motive of the universe. The lust after money which represented power. And yet who was she to criticize or blame?

Leaning back she looked at the prison which held her and which she had willingly accepted for the sake of the comfort it gave. The cell which paid off in her apartment, her salary, the power she wielded. Now the green-tinted walls seemed to be closing in, the air to carry a stale taint, the light itself a bleaching quality. Was it day outside? Night? Twilight or dawn? Only her clock could tell.

She stretched, suddenly thinking of the Kusevitsky Heights, the snow and the sharp, crisp air. The thermals would be good at this time of the year and the sky would be thick with gliding wings. Distance would take the cramp from her eyes and the wind clear the cobwebs from her brain. A break, the dean had said, well, why not? A short vacation and a respite from never-ending problems. Within hours she could be changed and at the Heights. The decision made, she acted with impulsive directness.

"Cleo? Order me a raft. Have it on the roof at my apartment building in an hour. Me? I'm off to the Kusevitsky Heights."

Where Dumarest found her.

The sky was alive with wings, blazes of defiant color which wheeled and soared to glide and sweep upward like giant, soundless birds. These were constructions of struts and plastic beneath which were suspended the fragile bodies of men and women, muffled against the cold, helmeted, their eyes shielded by goggles, gloved hands and booted feet making the wings extensions of their bodies. Adventurers mastering an alien environment, risking injury and death for the thrill of flight.

Myra thrilled with them, remembering the cold rush of air,

the near-panic as the ground had rushed up toward her, the surge of adrenalin coursing through her body as it had fallen away to leave only the vast and beckoning sky. That had been yesterday and, tomorrow, perhaps, she would glide again, but for today the sky was reserved for students under instruction and for post-graduates hoping to become instructors in turn.

From behind Dumarest said, "An engrossing sight, my lady. And a fascinating one. How can those who fly ever be content to walk?" As she turned he added, "If I am mistaken I crave your forgiveness but you are Madam Myra Favre?"

"I am. And you?" She nodded as he introduced himself. "How did you find me?"

"Your secretary was most helpful."

And unduly impressionable, but Myra couldn't blame her for that. Dumarest had shed the student's robe and now wore a military-style outer garment of maroon edged with gold. Fabric which replaced the robe's thermal protection and which did not brand him as a social inferior. A garb which enhanced his height and build, matching the hard planes and contours of his face, the cold directness of his eyes.

He said, "My apologies for having disturbed you but the matter is of some urgency."

"To me?"

"To me." He looked at the gliders filling the air, some casting shadows from their wings as they swept close and low, others hanging almost motionless against the sky like butterflies pinned to the firmament. "Is there somewhere we could talk?"

"You object to the Lion's Mouth?" She saw he didn't understand and explained as she led the way over the snow. "Obviously you haven't heard the legend. It seems that once, on a distant world, there was a cave on the wall of which had been carved the head of a lion. The carving had an opening between the jaws. Lovers would meet before it to swear their devotion and, as proof of their sincerity, those swearing would place their arms into the opening before they did so. If they lied the jaws would close and sever the arm." She paused then added, "That's why the cafe is called the Lion's Mouth."

It was snug and warm and built of stone with a low, timbered roof. Small tables stood on the floor and on each stood a gleaming lantern. On occupied tables the lights flashed red and green to the accompaniment of protestations and laughter. These were lie detectors, their sensors hooked to the seats, the colors revealing truth or lie. A novelty for the young, a useful furnishing for those who had reason to doubt their companions' motivations.

"You spoke of urgency," she said. "What problem is never that?"

"Death," he said. "The problem we all face but who hurries to meet it?"

She blinked at the unexpected reply and reassessed her first estimate of his intelligence. Not just a brash, well-dressed entrepreneur but a thinker at least. Why had he sought her out?

Dumarest shrugged as she put the question. "To talk. To ask questions."

The light had flashed green. "About the university?" She anticipated what she thought he wanted. "A position? You want to teach?" The light remained neutral as he stayed silent. "Do you appreciate the system? First you must convince me that the course you offer has commercial viability. Then you sign a contract binding you to pay the basic fees of the hire of a classroom or laboratory or what it is you need. The students pay you the fees you stipulate from which the university takes a percentage. In some colleges you would put the remainder into a common pool for equal sharing but we don't operate like that at Clyne. In any event, as a newcomer, you would have to prove your earning capacity before anyone would agree to share his fees with you. Am I making myself clear?

"Yes."

"All that remains is to discuss your field and to determine if you are qualified both to teach and to issue acknowledged degrees. That implies references—you have them?" She frowned as he shook his head. "No? Then why did you seek me out? Are you wasting my time?"

"I hope not." His smile asked her forbearance as his eyes demanded her cooperation. "Have you been at the university long?"

"In the bursary department? Six years."

"And before that?"

"I took a post-graduate course in bookkeeping and advanced administration." She saw the flashing green light reflected in his eyes. "Several years in all if you really want to know." It had been the major part of her life but she didn't choose to mention that. "Why do you ask these questions?"

He said, as if not hearing, "Would you have known the faculty? Being personally involved with them, I mean?"

"Not all of them—you must realize there is both a large static and numerous transient teaching population, but if you are speaking of the upper echelons of the Tripart staff then, yes, I know them fairly well."

"And ten years ago?"

"I was here then," she admitted. Her irritation had yielded to curiosity, why was this man so interested in her past? "What is it you want to know?"

"Did you know a man named Boulaye? A geologist?" As she nodded Dumarest reached out his hand and dropped something into her palm. "He sent you this."

She stared at it, not noticing the warning red flash from the lantern on the table, her eyes filled with the soft blue effulgence of the metal she held cupped in her hand. A nugget large enough to fashion a delicate bracelet or a heavy ring.

"Juscar," she said wonderingly. "So Rudi found his mine."

He had found it and lost it together with his life on the world of Elysius. Dying as his wife had died, as had Zalman, a man Dumarest could have called a friend. Lying crushed beneath the fallen mass of rock and debris which had created a mounded tomb. With him had gone the secret he had discovered: the coordinates of Earth.

The answer Dumarest had come to Ascelius to find.

"Dead." Myra shook her head, not in grief for the event was too old, too distant, but in sorrow that, somewhere, a part of her life had vanished. "Killed by a fall, you say?"

Dumarest nodded, it was near enough the truth to serve. "Did you know him well?"

"Well enough. We—" She broke off, looking at the lantern, mouth pursed in distaste. "Let's go somewhere else. These damned lamps remind me of watching eyes." . . . The eyes of censors which she could have hated as a child. Of their dictates which could have restricted her emotional development. Dumarest followed her from the table. The joke had turned sour or she had reason for concealment but the decision suited him. Of them both he had the greater need to lie.

"Rudi," she said, after they had settled in an arbor protected by curved crystal from the external chill, the biting wind. "How long would it be now? Ten years? Nine? Call it nine. I was younger then, inexperienced, perhaps over-attracted to the more mature male. Let's say he made me a proposition and I was too immature to assess it for its real worth. You understand?"

More than she guessed and Dumarest knew why she had left the table. Her time scale was all wrong and it was obvious why. Not nine years—nearer to nineteen. She had been young then and the rest would have followed. A fable to disguise her real age from herself as well as him—a weakness of feminine vanity unknowingly betrayed.

He said, "You were emotionally involved—is that it?"

"A nice way of putting it." She smiled and for a moment was what she must have been: alert, round of face, her mouth made for kissing, her eyes for laughter. The body would have been plumper then, the curves more pronounced, and she would have been hungry and eager for experience. "You are discreet, Earl. I may call you that?"

"Yes, Myra."

She stared at him, fighting her resentment, telling herself he was a stranger and couldn't know. Yet to take such a liberty! To be so familiar with a member of the Tripart faculty! Then, seeing his smile, she realized how foolish the reaction had been. How habit had betrayed her. If he had asked permission as he should, would she have refused him?

"Myra?" He was concerned. "Is something wrong?"

"No." Her gesture dismissed the incident. "A local custom. Something of a ritual, I suppose, but tradition dies hard."

"As do legends."

"What?"

"You told me of one," he reminded. "The Lion's Mouth, remember? And there are others." Many others but one in particular which was no legend but unaccepted truth. "What happened between you and Rudi?"

"Nothing. Not really."

"But you were close?"

"It meant nothing." A lie the table would have noted. "The forming of sexual relationships is a common pastime here on Ascelius. The strain of study, I suppose, of teaching. It was explained to me once that the creative urge is basically the same no matter how it manifests itself. An artist, creating a

46

painting, is subject to the same stress as a man attempting to impregnate a woman. The reverse is true, naturally." Pausing she added, "Are you always so bold?"

"In which way?"

"Familiarity?" She cursed herself for having mentioned it, for having now to explain. His expression as she did so gave no comfort. "You think it foolish?"

"Misapplied. I can understand the need for a barrier to be set between the faculty and the students for one must respect the other or nothing can be taught or learned. The same conduct governs the relationship of officers and men in an army. But I am not a student."

"True, but you aren't—" She broke off. Why did he make her feel so confused?

"A member of the faculty?" He finished the sentence for her. "Is that important?"

"On Ascelius, yes. If you want to be socially accepted by the upper echelons it is indispensable. Only academic ability is recognized." Her hands rose, fluttering, a gesture she hadn't used in years and wondered at herself for using it now. How Rudi had laughed at it. Dumarest, thank God, didn't. "What were we talking about?"

"Of Rudi." It was hard to keep her to the point. "Then he met Isobel?"

"She was young and new and ambitious. She listened to his promises."

"They married?"

"That's right. They married and left to find their mine and paradise. Now Rudi's dead and Isobel with him. End of story."

That was the end for them and for her but not for Dumarest. What Rudi had found could be rediscovered. If the chance existed he must take it no matter what the risk. Myra had known him—did she know more?

"Legends," said Dumarest. "Rudi was interested in them. Surely you must have talked about them? Shared his interest?"

"I had other things to think about. We weren't together all that often and when we were, well, other things came first. I'm sorry, Earl, I don't think I can help you. Is it important?"

She could never guess how much. Dumarest forced himself

to relax—to reveal his eager impatience now would be to ruin everything.

"Earth," he urged. "Did he ever mention Earth?"

Her laughter was the gushing of fountains, the clash of shattering crystal.

"Earth? My, God, Earl, do you share his lunacy? A mythical world somewhere in space. Find it and all will be yours. Insanity! A game they play in the common rooms when bored of everything else. Intellectual titivation with points scored for the correct progression of logical sequences. Guessing games which start in madness and lead to delirium. You should meet Tomlin, he's an expert. Cucciolla's another." Her laughter rose again, brittle with scorn. "How can anyone even pretend to be serious about such nonsense? Earth! The very name is idiotic!"

This reaction Dumarest had heard often before, but like the others, Myra was wrong. Earth existed. He had been born on the supposedly mythical world. To find it again was the reason for his existence.

He said, "Tomlin? Cucciolla?"

"Members of the Tripart faculty." She sobered at his expression. "Earl?"

"I need to meet them," he said. "Them and any others who were close to Rudi. Could you arrange it?"

"Perhaps." Her eyes grew calculating, studying him as if he were part of an elaborate equation, assessing, evaluating, coming to a decision. "There are various social gatherings and a party will be held soon. I could take you." She paused then added quietly, "In the meanwhile you could be my guest."

Chapter Four

Someone with a taste for the bizarre had decorated the room with skulls and bones, death masks and symbols culled from ancient graves. The music matched the decor: wailing threnodies which stung the ears and sent ants to crawl over the skin; mathematical discords set in jarring sequences which created unease and irritation. A condition aided by the glare of strobotic lighting which threw faces into unreal prominence with various shades of livid color.

"Myra! How good to see you!" A woman called from the door and came thrusting toward them, eyes flashing toward Dumarest before returning to his companion. "So this is your friend. Such a handsome man. Your new protégé, I hear. You must introduce me."

Jussara made her usual late entrance, demanding attention. Flaunting her feminity with a sequined gown cut and slashed to display the chocolate expanse of her breasts and thighs. Her teeth were plated with metal cut in a diffraction grating which filled her mouth with rainbows as the lights flashed.

"A professor?" Her eyebrows rose a trifle. "He is to teach?"

"Dumarest holds a doctorate in martial arts," explained

Myra. This story, she had insisted, would give him the status necessary to be treated as an equal. "We are investigating the possibility of his joining the faculty."

"And, in the meantime, he shares your home." Jussara's smile held malice. "Such a convenient arrangement and no wonder that you look so well. I'd thought it was because you had resolved your difficulties. Okos, I presume?"

"No."

"Well it doesn't matter as long as things have sorted themselves out. And, as for the new project—well, let's hope you are more successful this time." She looked at Dumarest. "We must talk again. If you can't reach agreement with Myra, I could, perhaps, find a place for you at Higham. I'm certain you'd be happy with us."

Her tone left no doubt as to her meaning. Dumarest smiled and said, "Thank you, my lady."

"So formal!" Her smile was dazzling. "Call me Jussara—who needs more than one name? Until later then, Earl. I shall anticipate our next meeting." Her eyes moved on to search the crowd. "Ceram! How nice to see you, darling! Be an angel and get me a drink. How is Toris this evening?"

She moved off and Myra helped herself to a drink, downing it at a gulp, wondering at her irritation. Jussara was a troublesome bitch who loved to deal in scandal and would throw herself at Dumarest for no other reason than that he was her companion. Would it matter if she did? If his taste was so crude she was welcome to him.

She saw his eyes as she reached for a second drink.

"You object?"

"Have I the right?"

"No man has that!" The sudden blaze of fury startled her and she gulped at the wine, feeling the sweetness of it, the after-sharpness which constricted her throat. An illogical reaction to a harmless question, the question itself a product of her own stupidity. Why ask if none had the right? "I'm sorry. That bitch always manages to upset me. Do you like her?"

"Does it matter?" Dumarest took the empty glass from her hand. "What did she mean about you having resolved your difficulties?"

"An adjustment which needed to be made. University business. A matter of balancing classes and courses and student enrollments. Sometimes it isn't easy but it's all done

50

now." She looked to where couples moved in complex gyrations. "Do you want to dance?"

"No. Where are the people we came to meet?"

"Later, Earl. Let's enjoy the party first."

He had waited long enough, forcing himself to be patient until this time, going through the pretense she had determined, playing things her way for lack of a better alternative. He was learning about the woman who had been so quick with her invitation.

It was a matter of cultural mores, perhaps; she had mentioned that the forming of intimate relationships was a common pastime, but had it been simply because she had been alone and bored and needing physical release?

Dumarest had begun to doubt it. There was a calculated deliberation in everything she did and even her passion was the result more of applied stimulus than released inhibitions. It was as if she followed the dictates of a manual, seeking reaction and not response, assessing instead of experiencing as if she were a programmed robot set to perform a routine task.

Now, again, the talk of delay.

He said flatly, "If you won't introduce me I'll manage on my own."

"A threat, Earl?" Anger blossomed again to burn in her stomach, to drive the nails of her fingers into her palms. "That's all you want, isn't it? Those damned introductions and to get them you'd lie in your teeth. Lie and pretend to love me and to use me as if you were doing me a favor. You bastard! If you were a woman you'd be a whore!"

Her anger shattered to leave a bleak chill as she suddenly became aware of the circle of watching faces, the silence which, too quickly, broke into a jumble of sound. Her coldness emphasized the realization that, to Dumarest, the insult had been devoid of meaning. In the world he knew the main ethic was to survive and to do so at any cost. And all were entitled to their pride; the woman who sold her flesh as much as the man who fought to entertain.

Different worlds, she thought dully, and how could she hope to understand his? Dumarest had killed, she was certain of it as she was in the manner it had been done. How had it felt to stand in a ring facing an armed man, nostrils clogged with the stench of oil and sweat and blood? She would never

51

know, could never know; her knowledge stemmed from books and not from the acid of living experience.

"Myra?" A man was at her side. "Trouble?"

Moultrie, big and tall and comforting in his strength, hovered now beside her in protective concern. They had glided together and he was proud of his physique, the body which gave him the confidence to glare at Dumarest, to attack him if she gave the word.

"No trouble, Roy. Just a little difference of opinion." She smiled as she touched his arm and wondered at her hesitation. Had she wanted them to fight? For Dumarest to be humiliated? If so the moment belonged to the past. "No trouble," she said again. "But thank you for your concern, Roy."

"If you're sure?"

"I'm sure." She smiled again. "Everything's fine."

He accepted the statement with obvious reluctance, and Dumarest guessed that Moultrie had wanted to press the matter. For his own aggrandizement? To gain Myra's respect? Or had someone put him up to it?

"I'll take your word for it, Myra. But you—" he glared at Dumarest. "I suggest you watch your tongue. A guest should have better manners."

If he hoped for an answer he was disappointed.

"Roy!" Jussara called from the far side of the room. "Bring Myra over here—I've a drink waiting."

"Coming!"

He led her away before she could object, leaving Dumarest standing alone.

The music changed; turning into a susurration of thrumming chords which faded to return like the pulse of waves on a shore. The stroboscopic flashes died to be replaced by a nacreous glow in which decorations shone with sickly fluorescence; leprous greens and purples beside scabrous reds and blues. The colors of blood and pus and gangrene. Of hurt and decay and disease.

Dumarest wondered at the motivation of the man who had created the setting.

"Madness," said a voice. "Insanity and spite and an infantile desire to shock. It's getting rather tedious." The speaker was small, round, his sparse hair combed in a fan over balding head. He held a drink in each hand and, smiling, offered one to Dumarest. "It's safe," he said. "From a private stock. Only a fool would trust what Levercherk provides at one of his parties."

Dumarest accepted the drink.

"I'm not a telepath," said the man. "I can't read your thoughts so you don't have to worry. It's just that your expression was obvious." He narrowed his eyes. "Did I offend you?"

"No." Dumarest took a cautious sip of his drink. It was fine brandy. "Are you a reader?"

"What?" The man frowned then smiled as he gathered Dumarest's meaning. "No. I lack that talent. To read a person from body signals and muscular alterations is a rare ability. But it required no genius to guess what you must have thought of this stupidity. Bones," he snorted. "Skulls. Masks and the rest of it. Is life so boring we yearn for its termination? Only the young can afford such mockery." He drained his glass. "Ragin," he said. "Carl Ragin. I teach at Clyne."

"Then you know Myra Favre?"

"Of course. And I know about you, Earl. A fighter, right? A teacher of the subtle means of destruction. A man who hopes to start a class in martial arts. You will forgive my bluntness, but I wonder at Myra even entertaining the idea."

"She's crazed," said a newcomer. "As mad as Levercherk but in a different way. Love, perhaps? It is known to steal away the intelligence." He stared at Dumarest. "Are you the cause?"

Ragin said, quietly, "Steady Dorf."

"If so she is to be pitied." Dorf, young, aggressive, confident of the power his status gave him, ignored the older man. "She could have given Moultrie his head. Well, if he cannot cleanse this place of the scum which has somehow crawled in to soil it, then I can."

"Dorf!"

"You side with him, Carl?" The young man made no attempt to mask his contempt. "Such strange company for a man of academic standing to keep." Then, to Dumarest. "I assume you will be leaving now."

Dumarest looked at the glass in his hand, the brandy it contained. A weapon as was the knife in his boot but to use either would be to make a mistake. These people would have nothing but contempt for a man who argued with his muscles. Moultrie would have been forgiven both for his status and his protection to a member of the faculty had it come to physical combat. Now, if he should accept Dorf's challenge, he could destroy any chance he had of gaining the information he wanted.

He looked up, conscious of watching eyes, the tension coiled in the air.

"You are courteous," he said to Dorf. "And I thank you for the opportunity to demonstrate the skills I hope to teach. I drink to your continued good health."

As he lifted the glass someone chuckled, an expression of mirth quickly silenced, but it was enough to tell Dumarest his guess had been right. Dorf was testing him, trying to make him display anger, a fighting rage. He was unaware of the danger he stood in, the risk he ran.

Now he said, "You must be as mad as the rest. What do you mean—a demonstration? Are you going to kill me to close my mouth? To avenge some imagined slight to your pride? To prove the superiority of brawn over brain? Is that all you have to offer?"

"No." Dumarest lowered the glass, feeing the burn of brandy in his mouth. "Now let me ask you a question. You take people, youths, men, women and girls of all kinds, and you teach them and give them a paper saying they have reached a certain standard and then send them away to live as best they might. But what good are your degrees if they need to survive on worlds hostile to learning? On worlds which have no place for the skills they possess?"

"You claim to be able to give them the ability to survive?"

"I teach martial arts."

"Warfare." Dorf shook his head. "The trick of murder."

"No!" Dumarest was sharp. "I talk of art not assassination. Of protection not persecution."

"Protection?" Dorf looked around, enjoying his moment of triumph. "Words. What the hell could you do if I came at you with a gun?"

"Came at me?" Dumarest shrugged, it was his turn to act the academic. "Exactly what do you mean? If you came running toward me carrying a gun? If you wanted to hit me with one? If you wanted to give me one? How can I answer unless you are precise?"

"I mean this!" Dorf snatched a roll from a plate; bread fashioned in the shape of a bone, his fingers closing around it as he swung to point it at Dumarest as if it were a gun. "Now, tell—"

He broke off, staggering back to hit the edge of a table, to fall in a shower of comestibles, as Dumarest, taking two steps forward, snatched the roll from his hand as he sent the heel of his other palm up and against Dorf's jaw. A blow hard enough to shock, to throw the other off-balance, but restrained enough to do no damage other than minor bruising.

"I'd do that." Dumarest threw aside the broken crust. "And that is one lesson you may have without cost: never give your opponent the luxury of choice. If he has a gun pointed at you then assume he intends to use it. Act as if he will and act without delay. Of course," he added, dryly, "it's best never to get into that position in the first place."

Ragin said wonderingly, "You could have killed him. Even if he'd been holding a real gun you could have taken his life. Damn it, man, I didn't even see you move."

"Training."

"Just that?"

"Add anticipation and execution. If you want to know more then join my course if and when it starts." Dumarest looked at Dorf who rose, hugging his jaw. "That goes for you, too, youngster. In the meantime remember not to start what you can't finish."

The advice stung more than the blow but was accepted where physical argument was not. As he moved away a woman who had been watching said, "You've made an enemy, Earl. Dorf has powerful connections and won't hesitate to use them."

"It was a game," said a man at her side. "Surely he accepts that?"

"It started as a game," she agreed. "It ended with his being shamed. Well, Earl, you've been warned."

She moved away, the man with her, others following to leave Dumarest in a cleared space with only Ragin at his side.

"So much for popularity, Earl, but Enid was right. A pity. You would have livened things up."

"I haven't gone yet."

"But you will." Ragin was shrewd. "I've a feeling about

you, Earl. The academic life isn't for you. It's too petty, too limited. There's too much spite and too much fear. Take Enid, now. If her contract were terminated where could she find other employment? Look around—they're all in the same position."

And all from the same mold—students who had graduated to stay on and take post-graduate studies and then to become assistants and gain doctorates and gain a professorial chair; prisoners in a system which fed on itself to create more; academics lacking the spirit or courage to break free of the surrogate womb and blinding themselves to the reality beyond the university walls.

Yet at least one had managed to break free.

Ragin frowned when Dumarest mentioned him. "Rudi? Rudi Boulaye? You knew him?"

"Did you?"

"To my cost I admit it. I donated a hundred vell to his crazy enterprise. Well, I wasn't alone. Tomlin had a share and Seligmann—he's dead now. Collett put in a thousand but he could read the writing on the wall and it was his only hope. Dying," he explained. "Rotting inside. All his money could buy him was drugs to ease the pain so he gave all to Rudi and went into freeze. That was a long time ago and when they tried to revive him it was wasted effort."

"Cucciolla?"

"He was against it and with reason but I have a suspicion he chipped in just the same. Another romantic who wanted to believe the impossible could be true and that legend needn't be all lies. But Rudi made it all sound so logical. He always was a persuasive bastard as Myra could tell you, but, on second thought, you'd better not ask. You knew him, you say?"

"He's dead." He added, "Isobel too."

"A pity." Ragin looked around and found glasses filled with streaked amber fluid. Emptying a couple, he refilled them from a flask he took from his pocket. "A toast," he said, handing one to Dumarest. "To the last journey."

It was the same brandy that he had tasted before and Dumarest took enough in his mouth to perfume his breath.

"A dreamer," mused Ragin. "A fool in many ways but show me an idealist who isn't. Weak too, but does that matter if you're lucky? Rudi had a way with women and Isobel was an angel." He sniffed and poured himself more brandy. Lifting his glass he said, "Well, Earl, let's drink to the death of a dream."

"It wasn't a dream," said Dumarest. "Rudi found his mine."

"Mine? Who the hell is talking about a mine?" Ragin shook his head. "I'm talking about the search he made before he left to make his fortune. The thing I and Tomlin and Cucciolla and all the others had shares in. The search for Earth," he explained. "Rudi swore he knew how to find it."

They had called it the Forlorn Endeavor and of them all only a handful were still alive.

"Time," said Cucciolla. "The years take their toll and many of us were old at the instigation. You've heard of Seligmann?" He glanced at Ragin as he nodded. "I see Carl has told you. He was dying at the time and the only real difference was he knew it. Consciously knew it, I mean, others refused to admit the possibility. Pantoock, Klugarft, Kepes, Bond—the list is long, my friend. Gone now. All dead and dust and ashes. Sometimes I think I hear their voices in the wind."

Calling him to join them, perhaps, for Cucciolla, too, was old. He moved slowly about the room, taking care as he brewed a pungent tisane, lacing it as if the act of adding the spirit were of momentous importance. Taking his cup Dumarest examined the chamber, noting the small, telltale signs of poverty. Dust lay thick on the row of books standing on a shelf, each volume protected by transparent plastic. More durable were the cassettes and recordings, the models and spools which added their litter to the home of a man who had spent his life in the halls of wisdom. A man who now waited to die, glad of the company, the opportunity to talk, to relive old dreams.

"Tomlin should have been here," he mourned. "A pity he left two months ago for the eastern peninsula. His health," he explained. "The sea air will do him good and he is lucky enough to have a son willing to share his home."

"And the rest?"

"Zara's teaching at a small school to the north. Nyoka is on a sabbatical—and he'd be a fool to return. Luccia—" The old man shrugged. "I'm the only one available, Earl. I and Ragin, who was one of the youngest at the time. As I remember it Rudi asked you to go with him, Carl. For some reason you refused."

"A moment of sanity." Ragin looked up from his cup, scented vapor wreathing his face. "I had a new appointment which would have been lost had I absented myself, and you know how hard it is to get a place with the Tripart. And, to be frank, I thought of the whole thing as a kind of joke. Earth—how can it exist? It's the same as Bonanza and Jackpot and Eden and all the rest. A name given to a dream of eternal happiness. You must have heard the stories, Earl. The legends. The world on which there is no pain or hurt or fear. The trees grow food of all descriptions, the rivers are wine, the very air is a perfumed caress. The sun never burns, the nights never chill, garments are made as needed from leaves and flowers." He drank some of the tisane, frowned, added spirit from his own flask. "The concept is intoxicating and we become drunk on wild hopes and fantastic optimism. To find Earth. To dip our hands in its inexhaustible treasure. To cure all our ills and slake all our desires. Paradise!"

Dumarest said, carefully, "Did Rudi actually know the coordinates?"

"I don't know. I don't think so but, as I told you, he was a persuasive bastard. He could talk the leg off a dog if he wanted. He managed to convince us he knew something and we backed him to follow it through." He glanced at the old man. "Some of us have reason to regret it."

"I'm not one of them."

"Not you, perhaps, but Luccia?"

Cucciolla shrugged. "Life is a gamble, Carl, as you must be aware. Some win and others lose, but it all evens out in the end. She doesn't regret the money she invested. Like us she wanted the results. She wanted Rudi to find Earth."

And he had.

He had!

Dumarest looked down at his cup and saw the shimmer of light reflected from the surface of the liquid it contained. Radiance reflected from the surging tisane as it flowed in a series of mounting ripples from one side to the other. The movement amplified the quivering of his hands.

Rudi Boulaye had cheated and lied for reasons he could guess. He had found the coordinates of Earth; the essential figures which alone could guide a ship to where it hung in space. The figures which were absent from all navigational tables and almanacs. Data which had rested inches from his hand and was now irretrievably lost.

Could a copy have been made?

"He returned," said Cucciolla. "He was absent a year or more and he came back and we met and he told us the bad news. Earth is a lie. It is nothing but a legend. The planet simply does not and has never existed."

"Yet you backed him to look for it." Dumarest was sharp. "You—all intelligent people—you believed the legend could be true."

"It was a game," said Ragin. "Something to amuse us. A childish fantasy."

"No!" Dumarest set aside the tisane and rose to pace the floor. Tiny plumes of dust rose from the carpet beneath his booted feet. "That's what you told yourselves after Rudi had returned to report his failure. An easy way of salving your pride. But before that, when you gave him your money, you had a belief in the enterprise. A conviction that he could succeed. Why?"

Cucciolla blinked. "Your meaning eludes me, my friend."

Was he deliberately obtuse? Dumarest said, patiently, "You must have had something to go on. Facts, data, items of information enhanced by considered logic. A rumor, even, which you considered to be worth investigating. For God's sake, man, think! Try to remember! Rudi went somewhere—that's why you raised the money. Where did he go? Why did he go there? What was it he went to check out?"

Talk, damn you! Die if you must, burst your heart, your brain, but talk before you go. Talk and tell me what Rudi had learned!

"Earl!" Ragin was standing before him, face close, eyes anxious. "Steady, man! Steady!"

"I'm all right."

"You sure? You looked like murder."

"It's nothing." Dumarest felt the perspiration on his face, the quiver of muscles, the raw tension in his stomach. He breathed deeply, inflating his lungs, fighting to be calm. "It's all right," he said. "I just want him to remember."

"He's an old man," said Ragin. "For him it isn't easy."

"You then? Can't you remember? You must have sat in on the discussions."

"Some, yes, but not all. I was almost a passenger and went along with the others." Ragin frowned, thinking, throwing his mind back into the past. "It began as a game, one of those what-would-happen-if things. What would happen if some of the old legends were true? Earth was mentioned, I forget why, and we took it from there."

"And?"

"That's about all?" Ragin met Dumarest's eyes. "All I remember," he added quickly. "It all happened years ago and things happened to blur the memory."

The desire to eliminate a mistake, of not wanting to appear a fool even to the inward self. A defense used by sensitive minds to maintain their delusions of superiority. Forget it and it ceased to exist. Think of it if you must but only as an amusing episode or a time of good fellowship, the meetings themselves the main reason for the existence of the group.

Ragin's reaction—Cucciolla?

"He had a book," he said. "Rudi had a book and it gave some hints and clues. Mostly rubbish, of course, but we applied the science of logical determination to the given statements and came up with some interesting speculations. As Carl said, it began as a game and progressed from there. Without Rudi to fire our imaginations it would have died within a week."

"The book?" A gesture told Dumarest it was useless to search. Rudi had taken it or it had been lost or destroyed. "The hints, then? The clues you mentioned?"

"I remember the first," said Ragin, glad to be of help. "Something connected to a religion of some kind. The creed of a cult which worked to remain secret. The Folk?" He frowned. "No, the People. The Original People. An item about a single home world. Ridiculous, of course, a moment's logical thought proves the inconsistency. How could so many divergent types have evolved on a single planet? How could there have been room to hold them all?" Those questions, for him, needed no answer. "But I think there was something else. A name. What was it now?"

"Erce," said Cucciolla. "It was Erce."

Erce—the name meant nothing. Dumarest looked from one to the other, at the books, the recordings. Had nothing been saved from those meetings?

"There was no need," said Cucciolla when he asked. "W

met and talked and thrashed things out but nothing was important enough to keep. As Carl said we were swayed by Rudi and went along with him. A desperate move on the part of some, admitted, but what had they to lose? And we trusted him."

That was a mistake, but Dumarest didn't mention it. There was no need to destroy their happiness with the past. Rudi had succumbed to greed but he hadn't been the first and wouldn't be the last.

"Erce," he said. "Are you certain about that?" He watched them look at each other, nod. "Was there anything else? Think," he urged. "At one point in your discussion the need for Rudi to travel must have been mentioned. You simply wouldn't have given him money for no apparent reason. He wanted to book passage, right? To where? He returned, correct? From where? You'd backed him and he must have made a report. Those places would have been named, surely?"

These would be clues to work on failing all else, and Dumarest kept at it long past the time when good manners dictated he should leave. It was past dawn when he finally emerged from the building into the street and he stood with the cold wind stirring his hair as it stirred the flags high above. Early as it was the streets were busy—the three-shift system of the universities had destroyed the divisions of day and night in the city.

In a cafe he drank strong coffee while thinking, half-listening to the gossip which wafted around and over him like windblown leaves.

"Another suicide in Bolloten's class." A girl relayed the news while chewing at a bun. "That's the fourth this semester. One more and I hear they'll terminate his contract."

"Someone should cut his throat." A man scowled over a bowl of gruel. "He pushes too hard."

"But teaches fast. Three years' work done in two. If you can't take the heat you shouldn't stand near the furnace."

"Hear about Pell's tussle with the bursary?" A man spoke over a mouthful of bread. "They were going to dump him when he came up with that paper on sensitives."

"Convenient."

"It saved his skin. Any guesses where he got it?" A scatter of laughter greeted the question. "All right, but only a fool would sign up with him for easy credits. In a half-semester they'll be valueless."

"I can't see that," protested a woman. "What if he did get it from Okos? What difference does it make?"

"None, my innocent, but what the Cyclan lift up they can also let down. What good is Pell to them? Take my advice and stay away from his classes."

A man said wistfully, "Anyone care to stake me to a dorm bed for the winter? Treble back when I graduate or I'll be your willing slave in the spring. No takers? Well, no harm in trying."

So spoke the voice of poverty, and it would be worse outside where students huddled together in the chill of the night dreading the bleak time which would leave many of them frozen in the gutters.

Dumarest rose and left the cafe, making his way to the field where he stood in a secluded spot watching the ships, the men gathered at the perimeter, loungers with no apparent purpose and no obvious means of making a living. There would be touts among them and students and those with time to kill. Others could be there for a different reason and he tensed to a mounting sense of danger.

A cyber on Ascelius—why?

The Cyclan could have little interest in such a world; their concern with graduates would come only after they had gained positions of authority. The universities themselves would resent the services the Cyclan had to offer, priding themselves on their own intellectual ability. Even the Tripart had little influence beyond its immediate sphere and the Cyclan were noted enemies of wasted effort.

A coincidence, perhaps, but Dumarest knew it could be fatal to assume that. It was time for him to leave and yet he had gained nothing but a few names, times, places none of which held seeming importance. This was scant information on which to base a search but it was all he had and all he was likely to get from those involved. There had to be another way.

Chapter Five

"Earl!" Sheen Agnostino smiled as she came toward him.
"It's good to see you again."

"You will help me?"

"Of course, but I'm not too sure of what you want. You
were a little vague when you called. The computers, you
said? You want to use the computers?"

"I want you to use them for me. Is it possible?" As she
hesitated he added, "It's a matter of urgency or I wouldn't
ask. That's why I don't want to use the normal channels—
there would be delay and I'd have to hire an expert and, well,
you know the system." One feeding on another and charging
as much as the traffic would bear. Cost he could meet but
time he could not afford to waste. "I'll pay, naturally, just let
me know the fee."

"Earl, surely you don't think I'm that mercenary?"

"I will pay." He was firm. He'd learned her financial condition as they had traveled together and was glad of it; now
he had a lever to gain her cooperation. "Don't refuse, Sheen,
on this world you can't afford to be generous." He delved
into a pocket. "Will this be enough?"

She looked at the coins, thick octagonals each set with a

precious gem, each enough to support her in comfort for a month. A dozen of them lying in the hollow of his hand.

"Earl, I can't—"

"There will be a fee for use of the terminals, right?" He knew better than to bruise her pride. "Please, Sheen, I need your help."

His appeal held more weight than the money he offered and he relaxed as, slowly, she took the coins. Money to ease her tension, to provide sustenance, to gain her a coveted position. To provide security and, for him, her aid now and her silence later if she should be questioned.

"We'd best go to the central node." The decision made, she was all efficient action. "I'll get you a technician's smock and you'd best carry a clipboard. Just look thoughtful and act deaf if anyone should talk to you. If you can't avoid a reply say that you're checking on the monitor system."

A suspicion verified. He said, "So records are kept?"

"Of course—how else to know the information flow and dispensation of charges." She added further explanation as, after seeing him muffled in a smock, she led him into the underground depths of the computer system. "At first each university had its own computer and data banks but it was decided that it would be more efficient to combine all resources. After all there is nothing really secret about knowledge and a data bank is basically only a library, so all gained by the pooling of facilities. Arrangements had to be made for the dispersement of income but that was a relatively minor problem. The main trouble came in arranging a feedback of resolved data into the general banks."

She talked on, explaining, acting as one colleague to another, her voice low enough to avoid being overheard by those who passed by—technicians, Dumarest noted, wearing smocks similar to his own. Mature men and women with a scatter of younger types who, like Sheen, were taking a postgraduate course. At a corner a grizzled oldster wearing the crossed flashes of electronics snapped, "Your business?"

Dumarest gave it, waited as Sheen spoke in turn, moved on as the man waved permission.

"A check," she explained. "Sometimes students try to sneak into the central node and gain the answers to various test papers. It means nothing."

Dumarest wished he could share her confidence. If the

man were efficient he would check, and if he did a record would be made. If nothing else, he could be evicted with his business undone.

"Here." Sheen paused at a door. "We'll use this terminal."

It was a screen above a keyboard set before a chair in a room painted a drab gray. The light did nothing to soften the bleakness. Dumarest looked at each corner, checked the rim surrounding the screen, finally leaned his back against a side wall with the door to his right. Sheen Agnostino frowned as he told her what he wanted.

"To track a man, Earl? His absences, journeys, returns? Is that all?" Her white teeth gnawed at her lower lip as she listened. "I see. Well, let's start with the name. Boulaye? Rudi Boulaye?" Words danced in whiteness over the screen to steady into marching columns. "Excellent qualifications," she murmured. "High reputation as far as academic achievement was concerned. All history, of course, he is no longer connected with the faculty of any university."

"But the records remain?"

"Unless erased, yes." Her fingers moved as Dumarest spoke. "Ten years, you say? Ten?"

"From twelve to ten." This was a guess but the time bracket should be wide enough. "He went on a journey and returned to take up his duties again until he left after his marriage about eight years ago." Unnecessary details, the entire known life-span of the man should be stored in the data banks. Dumarest scanned the words appearing on the screen, heard the woman's comment.

"Nothing unusual there, Earl."

Nothing—but there had to be more. Dumarest narrowed his eyes as he checked the columns; lists of classes, periods of study, absences, illnesses; the trivia of normal existence. An inexperienced operator would have wasted time checking them all but Sheen knew what she was about.

"A journey," she said. "He could have booked through an agency." The words flickered and changed on the screen. "Thirteen years too far back?"

"Check it out."

A long time but not impossible, yet if the man had found what he had been looking for how had he managed to restrain his impatience for so long? Another question to be added to the rest—another answer impossible to find.

"He took a ship to Karig just over twelve years ago." Sheen glanced at Dumarest from her position before the screen. "The only journey he took before leaving for Elysius about—"

"I know about that. How long was he away?" Dumarest frowned at the answer. "Ten months? Are you sure?"

"That's what the data says." Sheen touched more keys as she made a cross-check. "From time of obtaining leave of absence to time of resuming his academic duties a total of ten months eleven days." She anticipated the next question. "It would have taken six months normal to reach Karig."

Which meant Boulaye had never reached the world he had booked as his destination. Again Sheen, anticipating, provided the needed data.

"The vessel was the *Mantua*, a free trader operating on the fringe of the Iturerk Sink. It would have called at Alba and Cilen before reaching Karig."

If it had followed its posted schedule, but free traders followed profit not routine. It could have missed either or both the named worlds if Boulaye had paid high enough to gain a private charter. Or had the man left the ship at the first port of call? If he had then where would he have gone?

Ten months—in a sector of space in which suns were close and worlds numerous the choice was large.

"Earl?" Sheen Agnostino was waiting at the screen. "Is there more?"

"Check Varten and Hutz." Names gained from Tomlin and Cucciolla as planets visited while on the quest. Lies to add to the rest; neither could have been reached in the available time. Yet Boulaye had found something—where?

"Check the transit time to Alba," said Dumarest. "Double it and deduct it from the total. Halve the remainder and check on what worlds could be reached in the available time."

An elementary exercise but even as he gave the instructions Dumarest realized its futility. There were too many imponderables: had ships been available? Had Boulaye retraced his path exactly? Had he even left on the *Mantua* at all? A passage booked was not necessarily a passage taken as he well knew. A man, suspicious, hugging a rare and precious secret, could well have taken a few elementary precautions to avoid potential followers.

66

"Two worlds, Earl." Sheen turned to face him as she made her report. "Tampiase and Kuldip."

"Kuldip?"

"The closest." Her face glowed with reflected light as she turned again toward the screen. "You know it?"

"I've heard of it." He remembered Charisse, the Chetame Laboratories—could there be a connection? A moment's thought and he dismissed the idea—what would a geologist have in common with a genetic engineer? But what connection could Boulaye have had with any of the named worlds? What clue had guided his search? Where could he have obtained it? Dumarest said, "Can you run a wide-spectrum search pattern, Sheen? I want anything which could tie Boulaye in with Earth."

"Earth?" She turned toward him, her profile etched with light, but she did not smile. "Earth," she said again and busied herself at the keyboard. Words flickered to form a column. "Earth," she read. "Ground. The home of a small animal. An electrical connection. Soil. A mythical planet. The opposite of sky. Crude as in 'earthy.' To—"

"The world," interrupted Dumarest. "Check Boulaye with that."

A moment then, "That's odd." Her voice carried surprise. "There seems to have been a deletion. I'll try rerouting." Her hands moved with skilled practice as she explained what she was doing. "There is more than one way to ask a question, Earl, and a good computer operator knows how best to get the desired information. If you can't pass it then go around it or over it or attack it from the rear—ah!" She fell silent, looking at the screen. At the single word it contained.

"Erased," said Dumarest. "Everything?"

"Not the data."

"Then—"

"No," she said. "It can't be done. Think of a room," she urged. "One filled with a billion books. Books which hold the answer to every question you care to ask. If you wanted to build something, a raft, for example, they could tell you how. But you'd have to dig. One book might teach you how to temper steel, another how to cut a thread, a third how to weld. More would teach you how to mine for minerals, smelt metals, process the raw supplies. Then you'd need to discover the correct alloy for the antigrav units and how to make the generator and all the rest of it."

A lifetime of work and that was knowing what you wanted to begin with. But, once done, others could follow.

"Boulaye?"

"He erased the program," she said. "Whatever he was looking for he didn't want others to find." Pausing, she added, "I'm sorry, Earl. It's a dead end."

"No!" He had worked too hard, risked too much, come too far to give up so easily. More quietly he said, "Check it out, Sheen. Try everything you know. Perhaps there could have been an accompanying program, dual references, something like that." He waited as her fingers manipulated the keys, spoke again before she could shake her head. "Erce. Try Erce."

Nothing. She said, "It's not even listed, Earl. Is it a word? A name?"

A dream or a lie, something culled from a rotting book or a device to gull others—Dumarest thought of Boulaye, of how the man had died. Would he have enjoyed such a jest? Who would have known if he had?

The day had darkened with a bitter wind whining from the north, the air filled with stinging pellets of ice which settled to form a slick film on the streets and buildings. High above the flags streamed from their poles, ranked as sentinels against the sky, their gaudy hues paled against the leaden clouds. Soon it would be dark with manmade stars illuminating the heavens; patches of glow from serried windows, pools of lambence from lanterns, light which would mask but not remove the misery of those caught in the storm.

"Please, mister, I'm in the third year. One more semester and I'm home dry." A hand opened at the end of a swaddled arm. "A vell, mister. Just a vell."

A student at the edge of desperation or a beggar pretending to be just that; the voice was one Dumarest had heard on a thousand worlds, the whine as much a part of poverty as were sores and rags and skeletal faces. He walked on, turning into a narrow alley, leaving it to cross a wide avenue, skirted a bunch of students studying beneath a suspended lamp to watch others busy getting garlands on lines set high across the thoroughfare. The holiday gaiety was unmatched by the dou foreman who shouted instructions as he beat his hands against the cold.

"Tighter! Get them tight, damn you! Unravel that streamer and space the ornaments out evenly. You want to get paid let me see you move!"

The orders were fretted by the wind as were the flags and streamers, the garlands and gaudy decorations. Dumarest moved on, conscious of the grit of fatigue in his eyes, the ache of tension maintained too long. With steam and icy showers, hot blasts and relaxing heat he tried to get rid of them both, ending after the treatment lying on a soft couch wrapped in a fluffy blanket attended by an obsequious girl.

"You wish to sleep, sir?" Smiling she lifted the headband she carried. "An hour or a day it makes no difference. A touch and microcurrents will impinge on the sleep center of the brain and bring instant rest. The cost is small. For a little extra you could enjoy a sensatape attuned to the sleeping condition which will induce fantastic and erotic dreams. No? A tuitional tape, then? We have a wide variety covering a multitude of subjects." Her smile became more personal, more inviting. "Of course if you wish for something other than sleep that, too, can be arranged."

"Some coffee," said Dumarest. "And something to eat."

The coffee came in a pot decorated with shimmering butterflies, the cakes molded in a variety of shapes: cones, diamonds, hearts, loops, squares, tetrahedrons, all tinted in a diversity of hues. Luxuries Dumarest could have done without; the coffee was for the caffeine it contained, the food for its energy content. Eating, he thought about Myra Favre.

Why had she lied?

The men she had promised to introduce him to had not been at the party. Tomlin had moved long before and Cucciolla was almost housebound; things she must have known when she had so casually mentioned their names. Or had it been as casual as it had seemed? And why the invitation to be her guest?

Dumarest ate a cake and tasted mint and honey as he sought for reasons other than the obvious. She was not a creature of passion though she played at being passionate. A woman in her position with her influence would not want for lovers even if the partners she chose acted from self-interest. A reluctance to give cause for gossip? A possibility and he considered it, remembering the acid comments made by Jussara at the party. The spite of a jealous woman or a natural-born bitch—would Myra have wanted to avoid creating potentially awkward situations?

He drank more coffee, needing the stimulus it gave. Fatigue brought its own dangers; accumulated toxins could slow reflexes and dull the intellect and now he had to make a decision while knowing, inwardly, what that decision had to be.

If wise he would ignore the woman, but, unless he saw her, he would never resolve the one chance he had of finding the truth.

Outside the night had turned savage with ice crusted on the drooping garlands, adding a frosty haze to the lights as it sharpened the teeth of the wind. Dumarest walked quickly, following a memorized route, heading toward the tall building where Myra Favre had her apartment. It was high toward the roof, faced with a narrow patio edged with a parapet from which could be seen the loom of distant hills on a fine day, the glare of the field at night. At the street door he paused, wondering if she had changed the lock setting, but the mechanism operated and he stepped into enveloping warmth.

Riding up in the elevator, he wondered if she would be at home. He could have phoned but had preferred to arrive unexpected and unannounced. A gamble; he did not have access to the actual apartment only to the building; if she was out he had wasted his time.

A gamble he won—she opened the door at his ring and, suddenly, was in his arms.

"I was a fool," she said. "Stupid. But those bitches and Jussara—Earl, can't you understand?"

He said nothing, looking at the apartment, the woman standing before him. She wore a loose, one-piece garment which clothed her in glinting drapes from neck to ankle, the sleeves wide, banded at the wrists. The shoes she wore were thin and ornamented with sparkling gems. Her hair had been dressed in a style he had not seen before; locks touched with gold, set in sinuous waves, adding height and zest to her normal coiffure. Touches reflected in her makeup made her mouth seem larger, her eyes brighter. The artifice had given a temporary youth.

"You should have phoned," she said. "I waited for you to call."

"I was busy." He smiled and added casually, "And I thought you could be engaged."

"With Moultrie? Earl, must you remind me of my folly? Must I admit I was jealous?" Her hand rose to touch his arm, the fingers caressing. "Jealous and a little afraid. Happiness is such a fragile thing, Earl. A look, a word, and it can shatter into misery. Sometimes our own fear of losing it makes it happen. And some of us have too much pride." Her hand fell from his arm as she turned to where a table stood bearing a flagon filled with emerald and drifting flecks of ruby. "Some wine, my dear?"

It was new as was her gown, her appearance, the scent which hung in the air. Items bought to ease her misery or gifts for duty done? Dumarest remembered the greeting, the heat of her body, the pressure, the muscular quiverings as if she had exploded in a paroxysm of gladness or relief.

"You look tired." Again her hand rose to touch him, the fingers lingering in a caress, nails smooth and cool on his cheek. "I worried about you, darling. What were you doing?"

"Walking. Talking."

"To Ragin and his cronies?" Her shrug dismissed them. "Are you hungry? Shall I cook you something? Do you want to bathe?" Light flashed from the gems in her shoes as she crossed the floor to switch on a player. "Ieten's Seventh," she said as music throbbed in a low, passionate threnody. "Why don't you drink your wine?"

She had served it in a crystal container no larger than an eggcup set on a spiraling stem. Dumarest lifted it, let the liquid rest against his lips, tasted the ghost of fire and chill.

As he lowered it he said, "Why didn't you tell me you'd been Rudi's mistress?"

For a moment she froze, an image of glittering drapes caught in a fraction of time then, as fast as it had come, the moment had gone and she turned, smiling with her lips if not her eyes.

"Does it matter, darling?"

"Of course not. But it's a matter of mutual interest. Why not mention it as we're so close?"

"Perhaps that's the reason." She finished her wine and

71

stood twirling the glass in her fingers. "Anyway it was a long time ago."

"Twelve years," said Dumarest blandly. "Nearer thirteen. Just what did happen on that journey?"

"Earl?"

He said flatly, "Rudi booked passage on a ship bound for Karig but we both know he never intended to go there. In fact I doubt if he left on the *Mantua* at all. What he actually did do was to join you on the *Toratese*. Or did you rendezvous on Alba?"

A guess but a good one and he saw by her eyes that he had hit the target. This luck added to that he had gained at the last when Sheen Agnostino had gained the item of information from the computer banks.

"You shouldn't keep such things secret, my dear," he said quietly as he took the glass from her hand and poured her more wine. "What did it matter what you did or where you did it? A relationship—who could have denied your right?"

"A man," she said. "My professor at the time. His name is unimportant but he had influence and he wanted me and I was ambitious. And Rudi was wanting in courage—I realize that now if I didn't then. We were lovers but to him it was a game. He wanted company on the journey and I hoped to—well, what does it matter now? It didn't work out."

"But you traveled together?"

"Yes." She looked at her glass and drank and set it down empty to straighten and look at Dumarest with bold admission. "A game, he called it, and he played it as if acting a part. The passages booked, the separate embarkations, the later meeting in a hotel on Alba. Our honeymoon he called it—the bastard!"

She was a woman hurt and unable to forget the pain of the wound, the damage to her pride. A promise had been broken and her body used as a convenience by a man from whom she had expected love. This passion had been little more than lust when robbed of affection.

Dumarest said, "But you lived together. You hoped he would draw closer. You spoke of his hopes and plans and ambitions." His hope, the only one left, that Boulaye would have told her what he had erased from the computer. The clue he had gained—the answer, perhaps. "Myra?"

"We talked," she admitted. "Or rather he talked and I listened. You must understand the situation," she added as if it were of momentous importance. "You've seen Jussara and the others. You know how spiteful they can be. The academic world isn't a gentle one, Earl. It's dog eat dog all the way. That's why I had to be careful. A matter of self-preservation. You can appreciate that."

"Of course. What did you talk about?"

Her hand rose to touch her hair as if seeking reassurance as to her appearance. Crystal tinkled as she refilled her glass, the thin tintinnabulation blending with the pulse of sound from the recording. Emerald and ruby gave her lips the moistness of newly shed blood.

"Things," she said when the need to answer became a demand. "General things."

"Did he ever mention Erce?"

"I'm not sure."

"Try to remember," he urged. "Try."

Remember the nights and the whispers in darkness, the voids needing to be filled when desire had fled and only emptiness remained. When the ego needed to reassert itself and savor the sense of mastery and a joke could be enjoyed if a joke had been played. He saw her eyes veil with ruptured time and her mouth grow hard before she shrugged and laved her lips with more wine. She drank too much wine for her own good but it could provide the key to unlock repressed memories.

She smiled as he handed her more.

"Aren't you drinking with me, Earl?"

"Of course." A lie compounded with further pretense. "To happy meeting, Myra!"

"To love!" She looked at her empty glass. "Rudi never new what it was," she said to the crystal. "To him it was a joke—why else should he have laughed?"

Dumarest's silence was question enough.

"I thought at first he was laughing at me but it was more than that. He had nothing but contempt for those who'd trusted him. An educated man, a professor, taking pleasure in his ability to lie and cheat and delude." She looked up with a sharp movement to hold Dumarest's eyes with her own. "Erce? You said Erce?"

"You've heard of it?"

"I'm not sure." Her frown traced creases between her eyes.

73

"There was something like it—a scrap of legend he mentioned one night after he'd rutted like a beast. Erce? No—Circe. That was it. Circe. Something to do with an ancient who had turned men into swine. A woman, naturally, who else would be to blame?"

Dumarest watched as, again, she helped herself to wine. The level now was low in the flagon, small motes of ruby clinging like miniature wounds to the upper crystal, scarlet tears suspended over an ocean of green. She moved with the careful precision of a person who lacks true coordination over-reacting as the wine spilled over her hands, her laughter false and brittle.

"Green, Earl, the color of jealousy. Did you know I was jealous?"

The fruit of insecurity, of fear and hurt. Yes, he had known.

"As a child I did nothing but study. Learn and learn and learn all the time. Stuffing my brain with facts and figures until I dreamed of equations. A computer could have done better with far less effort and far greater efficiency, but my family was ambitious. Learn," she repeated savagely. "Deny yourself any pretense of childhood, sacrifice all your natural yearnings, eliminate all joys—and one day you'll win a degree and be rich and respected. Lies! God, Earl—how can they so torment a child?"

The glass snapped in her hand, the twisted stem turning into small spears which gashed her palm and sent red to mingle with the green. She dropped the shards with a small cry of pain, her lips gaining added color as she sucked at the wound.

"Let me see that!" The wound was nothing but his touch brought calm. He felt the quivering lessen as he wiped the flesh with a tissue, felt the heat, the sudden dawn of mounting desire. An emotion he did not share.

"Earl!" Her free hand rose to touch his hair. "Why do we waste time in stupid memories?"

"Circe," he said. "Was there more?"

The caressing fingers froze against his hair and her voice shared their sudden ice. "You prefer words to love, Earl? Talk to me?"

He said gently, "You spoke of ancients—let me tell you

74

something once told me on a distant world. To all things there is a season; a time to eat, to sleep, to taste the wine. A time to sow and a time to reap. A time to rest and a time to love." He paused while around them the pulsing music surged like the beating of muffled drums. "A pleasure anticipated is a pleasure doubled, Myra—or did they fail to teach you that?"

"That among other things—but since when has wisdom been found in books?" Her hand lowered from his hair and she turned again to the wine, shrugging as she saw the broken glass, turning again to face him, to look at him with a new confidence. "Wisdom," she mused. "You have it, Earl, the kind that must be learned and can never be taught. Kindness, too, so that you are gentle with a woman who lacks your strength. Compassion so you do not mock. Tolerance for her stupidities and, I hope, a measure of affection." Her eyes grew bright with unshed tears. "That, at least, Earl—do not deny me that."

The moment lengthened as the music came to an end, the sudden silence seeming to gain added dimension from the tension between them. The silence shattered as, from beyond the windows, came a sudden crackling and flicker of light.

"What—"

"It's the tests, Earl. The decorations—didn't you see them?" She was at the window before he could answer, the doors swinging wide to reveal the night, the small balcony, the railed parapet. More light shimmered on the frost and ice on both.

"Myra!"

"Come and look!" She smiled before stepping from the warmth of the room. "See? It's for the festival. The Luderaia—Earl, we'll have such fun! Look, darling! Come and look!"

The wind caught her hair, pressing the gown against her body as she moved toward the parapet and Dumarest saw her sway, one foot slipping on a patch of ice as she reached for the railing.

"Myra—be careful!"

He was moving as she stumbled, diving foward fast and low, seeing her turn, the sudden, startled look on her face, the eyes widening with horror as she fell back against the

75

parapet. For a moment she seemed to hang suspended on the knife edge of a balance and then she had vanished and he was left with the wind in his hair, a shoe in his hand as he listened to her fading, dying scream.

Chapter Six

Welph Bartain was tall and thickly built with a face schooled to mask emotion and eyes which held a cynical weariness. A man in late middle age, his hair grizzled, his skin creped with a mesh of lines engraved with experience, he was a captain in the proctor's department. He waved Dumarest to a chair after he had introduced himself, smiling as, without instruction, Dumarest set his head against the rest, his hands on the wide arms.

"I see you understand our procedures. Madam Blayne noted that you were cooperative." She had presided over Dumarest's second interrogation while a small, wasp-like man had conducted the first. Now, apparently, there was to be a third. Bartain smiled as if reading Dumarest's thoughts. "No. I am here merely to conclude the examination. I must apologize for the unusual delay but trust you have not been too uncomfortable. You have no complaints?"

"None." The guard had been accommodating; food and wine had been available at personal cost, books and tapes and means of passing the time on hand. For the rest the cell had been a place to wait, to sleep, to think. Dumarest said, "Why the delay?"

"The Ludernia." Bartain shrugged, his face dour. "It happens twice a year in summer and in winter and I don't know which is the worse. The cold makes students desperate but the heat affects minds in strange ways and always we are kept busy. Now, as regards yourself, the charge was made by three independent witnesses that you threw Myra Favre over the balcony of her apartment on the evening that the festival decorations were being tested outside her building. She was seen standing on the balcony. You were seen rushing toward her. She was heard to scream as she fell. Correct so far?"

"Correct."

"You protest your innocence?"

Dumarest said dryly, "I understood you to say that this was not to be a third interrogation. Surely you trust your machines?"

"A matter of routine. Please answer."

"I am innocent of the charge of murder." Dumarest added, "I am at a loss to know why I should be doubted. She slipped, I tried to save her but reached her too late. I have said that from the beginning."

"As I explained, this is a matter of routine." The officer picked up a sheaf of papers, apparently reading from them though, as Dumarest knew, his eyes never left the telltales set along the edge of his desk. "Dumarest," he mused. "You claimed to have a doctorate but—"

"I made no such claim. That was a pretense of Myra Favre's."

"A woman no longer young," continued the officer. "One vulnerable to attention and who would have been attracted to an intriguing stranger who claimed a mutual acquaintance. A person of responsibility who could help a man eager to make his way. Martial arts," he said. "An odd subject—did you honestly believe you would gain a large enough enrollment?"

"I've explained all that," said Dumarest. "But, since you put the question, yes. I believe that such a course would be attractive to those who come here for a quick and easy degree."

"And others who live in less gentle cultures." Bartain turned a page. "Why did you come to Ascelius?"

"For knowledge."

"And where better to obtain it." The officer's tone matched the cynicism of his eyes. "Or so those running our universities

78

tell us. Well, to get on—did you provide the emerald and ruby wine?"

"No."

A question he had been asked before—one of thousands repeated in various ways, set in different contexts, aimed like bullets or thrown like feathers. Probes to determine the truth of his story. The chair in which he sat was a complex lie-detector and the interrogations had been his trial. Were still his trial. The captain was obviously conducting a series of random checks. It was an hour before he dropped the papers and leaned back in his seat.

"You're innocent," he said. "But we had to make certain. Myra Favre was no ordinary woman—as a member of the Tripart faculty she was in a highly sensitive position. And there were certain unusual and disturbing factors—the wine, for example. You drank none?"

"A sip, maybe a little more."

"As your blood tests showed. If you hadn't been so cautious you could have followed her over the parapet. Drugs," he explained. "A mild hallucinogenic coupled with an euphoriac and, oddly enough, a strong sedative. A peculiar combination—you would have sensed a mild distortion of reality together with a carefree abandon and a mounting lethargy culminating in sleep. The abrupt change together with the amount she had drunk must have induced a momentary vertigo. The tension she was under could also have been a contributory factor." Without change of tone the officer added, "Did you love her?"

"No."

"But you were willing to stay with her."

"Yes."

"And not for the sake of financial saving—you have no need of money." From a drawer in the desk Bartain took an envelope and shook out its contents. Among them the blade of the knife glittered like ice, the chain of juscar like blue-tinted mist. Stirring it with a finger he said, "Portable wealth carried around a throat or waist. A mercenary's trick—your trade?"

"I've worked as one."

"And as other things too, no doubt." The finger touched the knife. "Madam Blayne reports you as being a dangerous man and I agree with her. One who would let nothing stand in his way. A man willing to lie and cheat and even kill if such things were necessary to gain his ends. If I were a curious man I might be tempted to wonder just what those ends could be?"

"Nothing which would have led me to kill Myra Favre."

"Nothing which caused you to kill her," corrected Bartain. "What you might have done is no concern of this office. We're not interested in speculation." He pushed the scatter of items back into the envelope and threw it at Dumarest. As he caught it the officer added, "But someone provided that wine."

Outside, the streets had the soiled, bedraggled appearance of a party which has lasted too long. Night would restore some of the gaiety with the sound and fury of electronic discharges, blazing shafts of color, drifting balls of luminescence but now, in the leaden light of the early afternoon, the streamers hung like dirty washing, the garlands like limp and flapping rags.

The people reflected the atmosphere. Students huddled in their dun-colored robes, waited impatiently for the festival to end and normal routine to provide the warmth of classrooms, the comfort of dormitories and dining halls. Those who could not afford such luxuries resented the others who robbed them of space and opportunities. Visitors ached from nocturnal enjoyments. Others counted their gains or losses and adjusted their aims. Some merely waited.

Dumarest saw a pair of them as he left the precinct station and turned to his left to pause and turn again to retrace his steps. These were two men, students by their robes, a little too clumsy, a little too careless. Dumarest studied them both as he passed; a glance which took in their boots, their faces their averted eyes. Men who could have been set as decoys to distract his attention from others who could even now be following him with greater skill.

Dumarest remembered the exotic wine Myra Favre had pressed him to drink. Something she had obtained to enhance the evening as she had obtained the gown, the services of a beautician—how had she been so certain he would return And why should she have wanted him to sleep?

"Mister?" The inevitable beggar stood with a hand out

stretched, his voice the inevitable whine. "I'm starving, mister. I've no place to sleep. If you don't help me I'll die."

Dumarest felt in a pocket.

"Me too, mister!" A girl this time, face sunken, eyes feral. "Just the price of a meal!"

More joined in, others came running as Dumarest sent coins spinning high, to catch them, to send them up again in a bright, enticing stream.

"Me, mister! Don't forget me!"

"No, me!"

"Me!"

"Me! Me! Me!"

Voices rose to a scream, restraint forgotten as Dumarest flung a shower of money into the air. Small coins spun and bounced, tinkling, to be snatched up or kicked or buried beneath lunging bodies. Another handful completed the confused scramble and, as Dumarest moved on, the pair he'd noted were caught up in the surge and swept to one side.

Had they been agents of the Cyclan?

Men could have waited in hope of easy prey—even though civilized Ascelius wasn't proof against thieves, and Bartain had mentioned the desperation induced by the cold. Aside from a scrap of overheard gossip Dumarest had no proof that the Cyclan were on the planet or that Myra Favre had been in contact with a cyber. It was time to eliminate doubt.

"Earl!" Jussara smiled at him from the screen. "How nice of you to remember me!"

"How could I forget?"

"You flatter me."

"No—I simply tell the truth."

"Which could be flattery in itself." Her smile faded a little. "I was sorry to hear about Myra. A tragic loss and you must be desolate. Why didn't you call me before?"

"I was otherwise engaged," said Dumarest dryly. "As you can imagine."

"The proctors—I'd forgotten." Her smile was that of a vixen. "Am I going to see you?"

"It is my dearest wish." He smiled in return. "Just as soon as I clear up a few things. Tonight if I can manage it. Are you free?"

Regretfully she shook her head. "Not tonight, darling."

"Tomorrow?" Without giving her time to answer he added,

"I'm too impatient and you must forgive me for being impetuous. Blame your own attraction. I forget I have things to do and could use some help if it's available. At the party you mentioned a name—someone you thought had helped Myra. Okos—if he's good I could use him."

"A cyber doesn't come cheap, darling. Why not try the university computer system? They are adapted to give analogues on stated problems. I assume you're concerned about your future now that poor Myra is dead. Did you actually see her fall?"

"Yes."

"And you tried to save her?"

"Of course, but that isn't why I'm calling. About my future, I mean."

"Of course not." Her smile turned cynical. "You must tell me all about it. Not tomorrow, but the day after? Can you make it then, Earl?"

"The day?" His tone left no doubt as to his meaning. "I was hoping to share dinner with you."

"That would be nice. Call me in the afternoon and we'll fix the time and place."

A smile and she was gone, the screen turning a nacreous white as the connection was broken. A doubt resolved but it brought little comfort. Myra had known the cyber. If she had seen him Okos would know of his presence, had anticipated it, perhaps, the prediction later verified. Was that why she had invited him to be her guest? Bribed to hold him in a silken snare? Did it account for the wine—lying in a drugged sleep he would have been easy prey. And why had Bartain held him so long?

He had phoned from a hotel and outside the streets were waking to a sluggish activity as shadows clustered at the foot of buildings and darkened the mouths of alleys. Dumarest plunged down one, took another, traced a wide-flung path of apparently aimless movement, finally plunging into an area of small shops and winding paths. In a store he bought a student's robe, picking one too large, worn, not torn but far from new. When next he hit the streets his face was shielded by a cowl, his bulk swollen by the voluminous garment, his height lessened by a stoop. His camouflage was less efficient than it seemed—putting a man into uniform does not make him invisible to his fellow soldiers. And aping a student meant he had to act like one.

"Not here!" A young man, hard, brash, his robe clean, bright with badges, held up a blocking arm. "This tavern's reserved for Schrier." He saw the badges on Dumarest's robe. "You don't even belong to the Tripart—this area's not for you."

Dumarest looked at him, at the pair who had come to join him. Relatively rich, spoiled, enjoying their moment of power. The owner of the place would tolerate them for the guaranteed custom they brought. To argue was to invite attention and worse.

He said, "I'm new. Just landed. Looking for somewhere to spend the night."

"Enrolled?"

"Yes."

"At Brunheld," said the youth. "At Nisen and Kings if those badges are to be believed. You'll find a place over to the west. Angeer's—they take anyone."

Dumarest moved down the street, masking his gait, eyes watchful from beneath the shadow of the cowl. Soon there would be a reawakening of gaiety with crowds thronging the main avenues in dancing processions, with women shrieking their mirth or outrage, men drunk and poised on the edge of violence. Thieves would be busy and assassins unseen. At such a time a wise man sought refuge.

Dumarest moved on toward the field, swinging away from it as the ships came into sight, heading north in the thickening shadows. The festival was ending—tonight was its finish. When the ships left tomorrow he wanted to be with them. But first he had to pass the night.

The woman said harshly, "You want more soup?"

Dumarest shook his head.

"Then out!" She jerked her thumb at the shelves lining the far end of the room behind the counter, the hourglasses on them. "You've had your time."

To stay he would need to buy more soup; a small bowl of tasteless swill, but if that was the cost he would pay it. He scowled as, delivering it, she demanded the money.

"A quarter? It was—"

"The price doubles after dark." Impatiently she snapped

83

her fingers. "Give! The heat's got to be paid for, the lights, the shelter from the wind. The bench you're sitting on, the table, the bowl, the whole damned setup. If you don't like it the door's over there."

Outside, the street was now scummed with ice, wind carried the burning touch of iced razors. A bleak area lacking the warmth of crowds, the shelter of massive buildings.

But, as a student, he was expected to complain.

"It's robbery. I'll report you to the university council and the student body. I'll have you—"

"Blasted and blacklisted and bedevilled—I've heard it all before. Now that's off your chest you staying or not?" Her fingers snapped again. "A quarter and no more argument."

He paid and lifted the bowl as she slouched back to the counter there to turn the hourglass. A woman with lank, dirty hair, a long, skinny body covered with a dingy gown, she matched the place she ran, the stained benches, the scarred tables, the uneven floor. The roof was low, the lights dim, other customers bulks of shapeless anonymity. Voices stirred the air like the rustle of dead and drifting leaves; arguments, discussions, the balancing of relative values as applied to certain teachers, the rare chuckle of amusement, the more common rising of an insistent tone.

"Pell has something, I swear it. The experiment was startling in its implications. He got his sensitives—you know that bunch of freaks he uses in his paraphysical studies at Higham —and directed them to apply their combined intelligence on the selected victim."

"A student in his class?"

"Yes, of course, but one chosen at random and the whole point is that the subject didn't know he'd been chosen. Well, after a while we all began to notice signs of abnormal behavior. He grew irritable, seemed unable to relax, made stupid mistakes. Then he grew terrified and swore that people were after him. A classic case of paranoia. And all caused by the product of directed thinking."

"Maybe." His companions wasn't impressed. "There are other explanations. I've heard of Pell and he isn't too reliable. He isn't above managing things so as to get a positive result of an experiment if he has to."

"You accuse him of raud?" The speaker snorted his impatience. "That's the easy way out—blame the man conducting the experiment and just ignore his findings. They were genuine, I tell you."

"But hardly as startling as you seem to think. It's well-known that one subject can influence another—any mental health worker will tell you that. One of the occupational hazards of dealing with the insane is the danger of distorted reality. So just what has Pell proved?"

"Induced paranoia by directed mental concentration. It must be obvious that the implications. . . ."

The voice died to a whisper as if the speaker had suddenly become aware of the others in the room. In a corner a man woke to the woman's prod, to gasp and fumble for a coin for the soup she served him. Stuff he didn't want and he slumped to snore again over the cooling bowl. When his time was up she would throw it back into the pot to be sold again.

A shrewd operator, thought Dumarest, watching her. The price fixed at just the right level. A quarter vell an hour—but in the winter the nights were twelve hours long. Three vell a night for the sake of watered mush and a score rested on the benches. Most would stay—for two vell they could buy space in a community dorm and get eight hours use of the floor, but they would get no food. And in a dorm there was no light by which to study.

He slumped, pretending to doze, thinking of Myra and the way she had died, seeing her face as she had fallen, hair and gown fluttering in the wind, the oval of her face a screaming blob as she had dropped to smash into a bloody pulp on the ground below. A woman misjudged, perhaps, she could have been nothing more than she had seemed, the wine a foolish prank or the result of ignorance. Yet for him to trust another was to place his life in their hands. And she had died too soon—there had been questions he'd wanted to ask, details he needed to know. She and Boulaye had spent time together on Alba as she had admitted, but she had returned alone and long before the man had resumed his duties at the university. Where had he gone during that time? What had he found?

Things now he might never know and Dumarest tasted the bitterness of regret. If he had asked while he had the chance, forced the pace, demanded her full attention—but to press too hard would have been to lose all. A woman sensitive, easily alienated, once she turned stubborn what could he have done?

Now it was too late and what had he gained?

A name, Erce, another, Circe, or perhaps the two were one, the first a distortion of the second or the other way around. This discovery was denied by the man who had later claimed to his wife to have made it—a claim Dumarest believed. The possibility that Boulaye had visited more than one world but no proof as to which. The attention of the Cyclan could lead to his death.

When would they strike?

He shifted on the bench as the night dragged on, easing his weight to avoid cramps, acting the part of a man sleeping and uneasy in his rest. There were shiftings as students left, their places taken by new arrivals who sat shivering despite the thermal protection of their robes. The bad turn of the weather would hasten the end of the festival. Near to dawn a crowd thrust into the room, cowled figures with snow thick on their robes. Two came to sit beside Dumarest, pressing close on either side, bringing the touch of blizzard cold.

"Soup!" one yelled then added, "It's bad out there. You could fall and freeze and never be noticed."

This was an unasked-for comment and Dumarest wondered why he had made it. Wondered too why the men sat so close. As the woman left after serving the soup he moved, trying to rise, to find himself trapped by the bodies which pressed against him. The bodies retched and doubled beneath the stabbing thrust of his elbows.

Outside wind and snow had turned the streets into a blurred and freezing confusion.

Dumarest ran, stumbled over a curb, fell to roll and rise wearing a white camouflage. From behind him he heard shouts, saw a glow of light quickly extinguished by the closing of the door, tensed as the sharp blast of a whistle cut through the wind. The men were acting in concert and he could guess why.

He moved on, head bent to avoid the driven flakes, boots padding on a cushion of snow. The wind was from the north and he headed away from it, letting it urge him south toward the field. An obvious path to take but it was a time for simplicity and those hunting him could think him too devious to do something so natural. At a junction wind, caught by the buildings, rose in a twisting vortex which funneled snow up and outward to create a node of clarity. In the pale light of imminent dawn Dumarest saw the waiting bulk of a man, another to one side, figures which advanced as he watched, hands lifting to point as if holding weapons.

"You there! Halt! We are proctors!"

Dumarest didn't wait to test this claim as he darted down a side street, plunged again into snow to turn at the mouth of an opening and again head south. The freak storm which had brought the blizzard ceased as rapidly as it had come and, when he reached the field, only vagrant gusts sent clouds of snow streaming like mist over the dirt and the ships standing on it.

Vessels touched now with masking whiteness, rearing like the towers of fantasy, some blotched with light from open ports, others dark, a few with men busy at their bases. Other figures, apparent loungers, but who would stand around in such weather and what was there to see?

Dumarest studied the ships. The nearest was locked and dark, that beyond had an open port with a couple of men inside, the one after had men busy loading bales from a snow-covered pile—work which meant the vessel was in a hurry to leave. Beyond it was a ship with an open port, the next had gaping hatches, the one after was dark.

To gain passage on any would take time but details could be settled once he was aboard. The one loading—an extra man among the rest could easily be missed. The one with two men? Added numbers could increase the chance of argument. One with an empty port could be the best choice—if he were given a choice at all.

Dumarest tensed as the whistle shrilled from behind. It sounded close, riding high against the wind. Gusts suddenly combined to create a brief resumption of the storm, sending clouds of snow over the field in a blinding swirl of whiteness—hiding the ships, the men, the figure of Dumarest as he raced from his position toward the field, the vessels he had noted.

Luck didn't last. Even as he reached them the wind died, distant shouts sounding thin, others, closer, loud with menace. A figure loomed before him, a hand lifted the club it held swinging toward his head. Dumarest dodged to one side, struck at the arm and felt bone snap beneath the edge of his stiffened palm. The man cried out and fell back to be replaced by others; shapes which became blurred with snow, seeming to vanish, to multiply, to be all around.

Dumarest spun, striking out, feeling the jar of flesh against his hands, the shock as something smashed against his temple. A club fell as he drove his fist into an open cowl, feeling the yield of cartilage, the warmth of blood from the pulped nose.

"Earl! This way, Earl!"

The voice rose above the wind, guiding him toward a blob of light, an open hatch, the figure standing limned in the glow.

"Hurry, Earl! Hurry!"

He felt a hand on his arm and tore free to race forward and dive head-first through the opening. He heard the port slam shut as he rolled on the deck, the rasp of locking bars as he rose to stare at the woman before him.

Charisse Chetame said, "It seems, Earl, that once again you owe me your life."

Chapter Seven

The sting was minor, a pain which came and vanished in a moment to be followed by a soothing coolness. Reaching up, Dumarest touched his left temple, finding a smoothness covering the area, the torn skin and bruised flesh left by the impact of the club.

"You are fortunate," said Charisse. "A little harder and it would have broken bone. Lower it could have torn out an eye. More to the left and there could have been shock to the interventricular foramen and the temporal lobe."

Dumarest said, "You know your medicine."

"Of course." She moved about the salon as a girl came to clear away the equipment—the same girl Dumarest had seen before or one just like her. As she left Charisse said, "Aselius—it has a reputation among students for hard teaching, but they don't know what that could really be. At three I slept with a hypnotute which poured data into my brain. At seven I knew every bone in the human frame, every major organ, the disposition of arteries and veins and nerves. And that was only the beginning. After that came the study of cellular structure, tissue classification, glandular excretions—the whole spectrum of living matter."

"Your father?"

"A hard teacher who had no time for anything less than the best." She moved to a table, a shelf, back to the chair at his side. The curve of her thighs tautened the fabric of her gown. At her throat gems winked in flashing scintillations. "And you, Earl? Did you find what you wanted on Ascelius?"

"No. How did you come to be there?

"Business. A matter of delivering some cultures to the medical institutes." She dismissed further discussion of the matter with a gesture of her hand. "It was the most amazing luck that I should have seen you and recognized you through the snow. What had you done to antagonize those men? Had they been hired by some jealous husband? A thwarted love or a rejected woman seeking revenge? And why didn't you use your knife?"

He said, "They have a system—trial by lie detector. Intent is all important."

"Of course. Had you drawn your knife and used it and killed you would have been guilty of murder. The intent to kill would have been inherent when you drew the blade. Not consciously, perhaps, but it would have been present and the machines would have revealed it. But why not just wound?" She answered her own question. "A matter of reflexes. Against an opponent the need to survive becomes paramount. Against a crowd that need would trigger the automatic basic levels of reactive response so you would fight at maximum efficiency. A dead opponent is a safe one—wounded he still presents a threat. Well, you are safe from them now."

For he was far from Ascelius and deep in space, wrapped in the cocoon of the Erhaft field and bound for Kuldip. Soon they would utilize the magic of quicktime, the drug slowing the metabolism and turning hours into minutes, weeks into days. A convenience to lessen the tedium of the journey.

He said, "I must pay for my passage."

"Naturally, but later, Earl. Later. For now let us talk. Did you learn nothing on Ascelius? Nothing to help your search?

Had he told her?

"Legends," she said. "When I was healing you that first time on Podesta you spoke of them. Of your home world and how you had left it. Of how you were trying to find it again. Delirium I thought at first but it made sense of a kind. Y how can a world be lost? Are you certain you haven't confused the name?"

"There are no listed coordinates," he said. "So no one knows how to reach it. And, no, I haven't confused the name."

"It happens," she said. "My father was interested in old things and he made an attempt once to plot the altering pronunciations of ancient words. Words like 'mother,' for example, and 'father.' They tend to move forward in the mouth. From the back of the throat toward the lips. See?" She pursed her own. "From guttural to sibilant—kiss me, Earl!"

It was as he remembered and yet oddly different. The fire was absent, the thrust of triggered desire, and he wondered at her reason for the caress. A proprietary gesture? A curiosity as to his own reaction?

"Just to remind you that we aren't exactly strangers." Her eyes held his own as she resumed her seat. "Now, to get on with what we were talking about. Take a word and move it forward in the mouth. It grows distorted, changes, becomes easier to pronounce if altered a little. The misplacement of a vowel or the alteration of emphasis on a consonant makes all the difference. In a few years the word becomes unrecognizable. Take Eden, for instance."

"Eden?"

"Another legend," she said, ignoring his interest. "A world, perhaps, like your Earth, but I doubt if it's as real. My father thought—you've heard of it?"

"Vaguely."

"A paradise, Earl. Odd how all these mythical worlds are claimed to be that. Legend has it that Mankind started in Eden. That it was owned by some kind of goddess and that she lost her temper and threw everyone out when they offended her. If anything at all the story has to be allegorical but that isn't the point I'm trying to make. My father thought that Eden had to have been 'Garden.' You see? A simple change and an ordinary word becomes something novel."

He said, "Was your father really interested in old legends?"

"Yes, really. There are old books at home, records and such. He used to value them and spend hours studying them. You can examine them if you like."

"A promise?"

"Of course." Bored with the subject she changed it. "Earl, do you remember how we parted?"

After the frenzy came a period of calm during which he must have slept. The serving girl had ushered him from the vessel.

"I remember," he said dryly. "It was a little abrupt."

"Maybe too abrupt. I've thought about it often and wondered if I'd made a mistake. Business," she added bitterly. "I had the beast to deliver and things to take care of. I didn't realize just how unusual you really are. Why are we always in so much of a hurry?"

He shrugged, not answering, looking at the flashing splendor of her necklace. Remembering the other gems she had worn, points of light which had winked in her hair. A trait she seemed to favor and he wondered at the idiosyncrasy. The scintillation drew attention from her face and eyes, her lips and cheeks, an effect most women would regard as detrimental. Jewels were normally used to accentuate, not rival, natural charms.

"You look pensive, Earl." Her hand lifted to touch his cheek. "The wound troubling you?"

"No. It's fine."

"Something else, then?" Her smile encouraged his confidence. "Disappointed, perhaps?"

"A little, yes."

"At the wasted journey, I understand. And you must be tired." The touch of her fingers became a caress. "So very tired. The fight and the shock of your injury and I'll bet you had no sleep—what else can you expect?"

"I'm fine." A lie; the fatigue she had mentioned was gritting his eyes and dulling his vision. He resisted the desire to yawn. "I'll be all right."

"Of course you will." Her hand fell from the nape of his neck. "Natural sleep is the best medicine there is. Your cabin has been made ready." She rose, waited for him to join her, smiled as she led the way to the door. "I'll take you to it and Earl—you are safe now. There is no need to lock your door."

There had been a face which had smiled at him and touches which had felt like the impact of snow before they turned to flame but he had been too tired to notice and had ignored them to wander like a ghost in a haunted land of dreams. Now, awake, he lay supine and looked at a ceiling decorated with writhing serpents. At walls bearing the snarling faces of assorted beasts. At the bed on which he rested in naked comfort.

Luxury matched by the thick carpet, the glowing plates set to provide a softly warm illumination, the rest of the furnishings.

Visible proof of the wealth of the Chetame Laboratories.

Of Charisse who owned them.

Leaning back, he remembered their conversation. The collection of old books and records her father had studied and of the legends he had wanted to pursue. Eden—he knew of several worlds named that, but had there, at one time, been a single spot as Charisse had said? A garden—if the word had changed that's all Eden could mean. And Earth?

He tried it, mouthing the word, advancing it toward his lips, noting the increasing difficulty in pronouncing it aloud. The hiss which came when trying to push the diphthong too far. The change.

Earth ... Earse ... Earce ... Erce ...

Erce?

Erce!

The name Boulaye had gained from an old book or so he had claimed. Another name for Earth? An older one?

Where had the man gone after he'd left Myra Favre on Alba?

Dumarest rose to pace the floor, trying to flog himself into action. A shower stood in a corner of the room and he stepped into it, ice-cold water lashing from jets to wake his flesh from lethargy.

An old book—how long would a book last on Ascelius unless protected from biodegradation? A copy, then, but from where?

The sting of water ceased and he dried himself before looking into a mirror. It was of tinted glass, designed to flatter, lessening the harshness of mouth and eyes. The dressing on his temple had diminished a little; the compound absorbed into his flesh. A mote of darkness rested beneath the transparency at the healing lip of the wound.

Turning, he searched for his clothes, finding them in a cabinet. Dressed, he sat on the edge of the bed and stared thoughtfully at the writhing decorations on a wall. He felt

93

that he trembled on the edge of a discovery but it eluded him as had the identity of the face in his dream. Myra? Charisse? Isobel Boulaye?

Would her husband's ghost never be at rest?

The man had come into possession of a book, common currency among students. Could one of them have given it to him in return for a favor received? Or mentioned something which had aroused his interest? Caused him to send for a copy, but if so, from where? And what had been the trigger to send him on his journeying? Erce? Erce—and something else. What had Myra said before she died? A word her lover had mentioned in laughter.

A clue?

Dumarest rose and stepped toward the door. It opened at his touch and he passed from the cabin into the passage. It was deserted, the air holding a strange, acrid taint at variance with the ornamentation. There should have been perfume, the odor of incense, rich and decadent smells to match the opulence. Beneath his boots the deck was covered with soft fabrics which muffled his tread. As he neared the forepart of the vessel a uniformed man stepped forward to bar his way.

"I'm sorry, sir, but this is a restricted area."

"I'm a guest of Charisse Chetame."

"I know you are, sir." The man was big with the easy confidence of a man who knew his own capabilities. "The restriction remains."

Dumarest said quietly, "I was only identifying myself. I would appreciate the loan of some star charts of this area together with an almanac and measuring devices."

"Sir?"

"A problem I wish to resolve." Dumarest added, "A hobby of mine and it will serve to pass the time. I would appreciate your cooperation."

The guard barely hesitated; a guest of the owner would have influence and his request was harmless enough. "It will be my pleasure to help, sir. This area, you say? I'll have them sent to you in the salon."

Dumarest nodded, turned, walked back down the passage toward where the engine room would be, the cargo holds, the generator. Another guard materialized to stand before him.

"I'm sorry, sir—"

"I know," said Dumarest. "This area is restricted."

"That is correct, sir." The man could have been the twin of the other guard. He added, "Aside from the control section and the private cabins the rest of the vessel is free."

"The salon?"

"Yes, sir, of course."

Like the cabin it was extravagently decorated with the likeness of beasts, birds, things which crawled. It was deserted, the charts and things Dumarest had asked for lying heaped on the table. Sitting, he adjusted them, unrolling the charts, holding them fast with magnetic clips, checking the almanac, placing the protractors and dividers, the rules and scales close to hand. An astrogator would have done it faster, an engineer as well, but he was capable enough.

And Sheen Agnostino had narrowed the field.

Boulaye had been on Alba with Myra Favre and he knew the time of their official honymoon. Knew too the time she had returned and so the period the man had available for journeying. Alba was a busy world set close to suns and teeming planets; Tampiase, Cilen, Elgent, Kuldip, Chord, Freemont—all would have been within reach.

Dumarest sat back, looking at his notes, the charts, the almanac which gave stellar positions at definite times. Stars moved and so did their worlds and that movement affected journey times. A thing he'd needed to check as he had others: Boulaye's character, his determination, his resources.

A man basically weak who wanted to gain with the minimum of effort. One easily swayed. One with a twisted sense of humor; a sadistic bent which could have stemmed from a knowledge of his own inadequacy.

Which world had he visited? On which had he learned where Earth was to be found?

Again he felt himself to be on the edge of a discovery and yet lacking the ability to take the one step which would make things clear. Tampiase? A possibility, but if he had visited it Boulaye would have had little time and what was so special about the world? Elgent? A place of sands and winds—eliminate Elgent. Chord? There was a cult of ancestor worship which turned the cities into necropolises. A promising situation for a man who had learned an old and ancient name for the planet Earth. Had he gleaned a clue in some esoteric ritual? Deciphered some fading inscription?

Dumarest closed his eyes, wondering at his bafflement. Not

at the inability to solve the problem but at the fog which seemed to cloud his memory. The word Myra had said she had heard while lying at her lover's side. Not Erce—of that he was certain. One which had sounded like it and which he'd taken for a distortion.

Opening his eyes, he looked at the beasts ornamenting the walls, the writhing depictions of life in many forms. Decoration inspired by the legend of Eden? The goddess which had ruled over a multitude of forms? What had Myra said?

Dumarest looked at his hands, the charts, the answer which had stared him in the face all along.

Circe—the woman who had turned men into beasts.

How better to describe a genetic engineer.

Kuldip was a small, dark world warmed by a distant sun; a smoldering furnace blotched with ebon, ringed by a scarlet corona. The mountains had weathered into hills, the seas dried into lakes dotted with islands and scummed with weed. From the hills men wrested ores, gems, precious metals. From the seas the product of massive bivalves. The main industry was the Chetame Laboratories.

"It's big." Dino Sayer lifted a hand, pointing. "The largest installation on the planet."

He was an old man, his body frail beneath his uniform of russet and emerald, his head bald, the skin seeming to bear a high polish. His face was seamed, lined and scored with the clawed feet of time, his eyes a pale azure, the whites flecked with yellow. A technician high in the hierarchy of the laboratory. The guide provided to show Dumarest around.

"It's grown," he said, his hand moving to point. "A century ago we only had that building, that space, those stockades. When Armand took over he engaged on a period of expansion and gained finance to put up the rest."

"Armand Chetame?"

"That's right. Charisse's father. A genius." Sayer shook his head in regret at the man's passing. "I came to him as a boy and he treated me like a son. Taught me, educated me, guided me every step of the way. Others, too, of course, but he was like that. He wanted to build the best team he could get and he set out to do it. I reckon he did it too."

Dumarest recognized the pride in the old man's voice, his proprietary tone. The laboratories had been his life and he would stay with them until he died. Dumarest looked over the edge of the raft at the long, barrack-like buildings, the warehouses, fences, towers, stockades. Animals grazed on lush vegetation, some looking up as the shadow of the raft darkened the ground before them.

"Prototypes?"

"Basic stock," explained his guide. "Ruminants, naturally, providing meat, hides, bone, horn—all the animal can be utilized. We adapt their germ plasm to various requirements as the need arises. Another of Armand's ideas—he figured it was better to have a selected basic than to develop from scratch at each order. For one thing we can fill a small demand and do it without waste of time."

"Yields?"

"That depends on the requirement." Sayer was pleased at the informed interest. "If you own ground on a rough, tough world you aren't interested in milk-yield as much as survival ability. You want your beasts to be able to live on local growths, withstand extremes of temperature, be agressive enough to defend themselves against predators and breed fast enough to show a profit. From the basic stock we can provide all that. Gestation is four months and a calf is weaned in as many weeks. High metabolic factor for the initial period slows after maturity has been reached. A hide tough enough to withstand fire, thermal fat distribution to withstand cold, coat capable of rapid moult and regrowth and so adapted to short seasons. You can freeze those beasts in solid ice," he boasted. "Keep them frozen for a month and, as long as they can breath, they'll survive. They'll grow fat where other cattle will starve."

Dumarest said, "Adaptive triggers?"

"Naturally. When food is short a sterility factor operates to reduce fertility. Climatic change can slow gestation up to double the normal period or induce abortion if the foetus is newly established—these creatures have been designed to survive. You a stock farmer?"

"I've worked on such farms."

"Hunted, too, I guess." Sayer nodded his satisfaction. "You ask the right questions and I guess you know your business. Over there, now—" He pointed. "Behind that grove of trees. We're trying something new. Armand didn't bother with novelties," he explained. "He went for the basic needs; cattle for

97

sustenance, beasts for riding, birds, fish, snakes, even. A snake can live in places a man can't and they make good, cheap eating. But Charisse wants to open new markets."

Dumarest remembered the creature he had fought. "For guards?"

"That and spectacle and for the hunting preserves. Take us down, Feld."

The driver of the raft turned in his seat. "You want to land?"

"No. Just take us down." Sayer pointed again as the man obeyed. "There! See?"

Beyond the trees rested long grass, an apparently lifeless swathe then, as Dumarest looked, he saw a long, loping shape, another, a dozen which reared to reflect the sunlight from pointed fangs. Dogs the size of ponies, their coats mottled in tawny camouflage.

"Guard dogs," explained Sayer. "A special order but we've found them useful for general patrol duties and are maintaining a stock pack. Their intelligence has been enhanced as has their group response. A pack will take orders and work in unison. Nothing really new in that, of course, dogs have been used to track and defend and hold and kill for millennia now, but we've increased their potential about as far as it will go. Want to take a closer look?"

The raft dropped as Dumarest nodded and he gripped the rail as, below, long bodies lifted to reveal the large, clawed feet, the well-muscled legs. The creatures sat after the initial leap, jaws gaping, eyes brightly watchful.

Dumarest said, "What if there were an accident and we crashed?"

"They won't kill," said the driver. "Not without a direct command. They'd just hold us until ordered to let us go by the captain. After dark it would be different." He lifted the raft a little as he spoke. "Then they have the kill command," he said. "No one can hope to break into the laboratory area."

"We guard our own," said the old man. "Vicious looking things, aren't they? Want to see something really unusual? Feld—take us to the teleths."

Another area, this time one set with circular huts, paths small patches set with various crops. Dumarest looked for signs of human life and saw small figures standing in the shadow of trees. Pygmies? He narrowed his eyes as the raft dropped, lowering to come to a landing on a patch of grass.

"No dogs," said Sayer. "And don't worry about danger. I'll take care of it if anything should happen."

"With that?"

"A stunner." The guide hefted the thick-barreled weapon. "Throws the nervous system all to hell. They have a receptor engrafted in the skull and attached to the main ganglia. Not that we'll need it. The things are tranked all the time."

"Drugged?"

"An implant which affects the higher nerve centers. We maintain it unless special tests are needed. But for now I want to show you something." Sayer paused and looked toward the small figures. "Now."

For a long moment nothing happened then a group of the shapes came forward to stand at the edge of the patch of grass. Not human though they had a humanoid form—monkey-like things about four feet tall with large, staring eyes, crested skulls, a fine down covering hides of mousey gray. Their hands were slender each bearing three fingers and an opposed thumb. Their feet matched their hands. All appeared neuter.

"Sexual development has been arrested at the prepuberty stage," said the old man. "Physically they are large, undeveloped children, but can be adapted for breeding if the necessity should arise. At the moment we are checking out a new gene pattern aimed at achieving a rudimentary telepathic ability. Now watch. I'm going to have them split into two groups, one will pick up debris from the paths, the other from the grass."

He fell silent and, as far as Dumarest could see, made no signals of any kind. The group moved into two units each doing as he'd predicted.

"Telepathy," said Sayer. "I'm thinking the commands at them and they are responding. We've adapted them from a form of life found in the forests of Chalachia and once we get a few problems sorted out there's a market waiting for all we can produce. Servants," he explained. "Soft, gentle, cheap—they can live on a bowl of mush a day. Life span about a dozen years from gaining optimum physical development. Easily trained and directed—just think at them and they obey."

"Why not just teach them to talk?"

"Impossible—they lack any trace of a speech center in the cortex. In their natural state they are just animals; arboreal types living on fruit and bark and nuts. The telepathic ability is a gene addition which gives them about the only real value they have." Sayer stared at those working and, as one, they ceased their labors and returned to the shadow of the trees. "About the last thing Armand instigated."

Dumarest said. "I thought he was strictly utilitarian in his developments."

"He was but this resulted from an idea he had about the Original Man." The guide smiled at Dumarest's expression. "No, I'm not joking. Armand grew interested in old legends and myths and came up with the notion that, at one time, there would have had to have been a prototype for Mankind. He figured that we had degenerated from the prime stock and that certain organs such as the vermiform appendix, the pineal gland and the dead areas of the brain must once have had a useful function. If that was the case then we must have lost certain abilities and he wanted to restore them. Telepathy was something he thought could have been a lost attribute."

"So he tried to incorporate it into monkeys?"

"He just wanted to see if it could be done. Once the gene had been isolated and stabilized he would have incorporated it into his master chromosome map." Sayer shrugged. "Well, he died before he'd barely started. A pity—he'd deserved the relaxation of a hobby. I guess he just left it too late." He looked at the sky, the sullen ball of the lowering sun. "Like we're doing. We'd best get moving if I'm to get you back to the house before dark."

Chapter Eight

It was a place of peaked roofs set with spires around which twisted serpents carved from emerald stone. Decoration repeated in the gargoyles which guarded the corners, the felines set between soaring pillars, the array of birds which perched in frozen immobility on the walls. A motif reflected in the interior with vaulted chambers and echoing galleries, wide stairways and floors graced with elaborate mosaics.

In his room Dumarest stared through a narrow, pointed window at the last glare of the dying sun, seeing the scud of low cloud burning crimson, the ground itself bearing the stain of spilled and drying blood. From somewhere came a distant howling and he remembered the dogs, the warning he had been given. It had been a warning, of that he had no doubt, one clumsily delivered but unmistakable all the same. To leave the house and to wander unescorted through the grounds meant death.

This was an odd way to treat a guest but everything had been odd since he had joined the ship on Ascelius. The turgid nature of his thoughts, the journey which had seemed too short even allowing for the convenience of quicktime. And after the landing when he had been given into the charge of

Dino Sayer and taken on a tour of the establishment which had lasted until now. A means of keeping him from the house? Of keeping him under guard?

"My lord?" The girl was the one he had seen before or her twin. "Your bath is ready, my lord."

"Thank you." He spoke without turning.

"Do you wish my assistance?"

"No." He turned, his smile softening the refusal. "But I thank you for the offer. Were you on Podesta?" He saw the frown, the sudden bewilderment in the wide, vacuous eyes. "Never mind."

The bath matched his room, the tub made from a solid block of marble, smoothed and contoured to cradle the back and thighs. Water fumed from twin faucets adding to that drawn by the girl, perfume rising to thicken the air with pungent smells. From the molding running below the high groined roof carved beasts watched as he pulled the plug, flushed out the water and what it contained, refilled the tub with steaming, uncontaminated liquid. Immersed he relaxed.

Had the girl been the same?

Had the perfume been other than what it seemed?

Had he been kept from the house to avoid seeing who else enjoyed the hospitality of Charisse Chetame?

The questions increased the burden of the rest and he mulled them over in his mind as the hot water eased his body and tensions. It was good just to lie and relax. Good to refrain from worry, to drift, to dream, to let events take their course.

Why had the journey seemed so short?

Dumarest rolled and felt the water rise over him as he engulfed his head to hold it below the surface as a fire grew in his lungs. This grew into an overriding need for air to burst as water showered and he rose, gasping, chest heaving, steam rising from his body as he stepped from the tub to stand before a mirror. Vapor misted it and he cleared it with the edge of his palm.

Intently he examined his temple.

The wound had healed. the transparent covering replaced by a smooth expanse of skin marred only by an ebon fleck. A point of blackness he had seen before, but then it had rested close to the edge of damaged tissue. Tissue which had healed too fast. A clock which proved the journey had taken longer than it had seemed.

Drugs?

They would account for it; inducing long periods of sleep which he would imagine to be times of normal rest. But he had eaten little and that only the usual basic drawn from a communal spigot. Charisse had remained absent after their first meeting when she had dressed his wound. Water, like food, had come from a communal faucet. The air had been shared. What else remained?

Lifting his hands, he touched the point of darkness on his temple and felt something hard. Setting the nails of his thumbs to either side of the mote, he pressed as he squeezed them together. A touch of pain then the ebon fleck lifted to be caught on a thumbnail and carried to the level of his eyes. A small cylinder of something hard and gritty which had rested in his flesh like a splinter of wood.

He dropped it into the bowl and flushed it with a stream of water. The pressure of his nails had left small, angry indents to either side of a spot of crimson. More water washed away the blood and he massaged the flesh to remove the indents. Some redness remained as did the tiny wound and he stooped to search the side of the bath where it joined with the floor finding, as he'd expected, traces of dirt. A touch and the wound was sealed with dirt, fresh blackness simulating the implant. As he turned from the mirror he heard the scuff of sandals from the room outside and cried out as he hit the side of the tub with the heel of his hand.

"My lord?" The girl came running, eyes searching the bathroom. "Are you hurt?"

"No."

"I heard—"

"I slipped." Dumarest lifted the hand he'd held to his temple. "Banged my head a little. It's nothing serious."

She examined him, "Just a little red, my lord. You were fortunate. Should I summon medical aid? Bring you astringents and ice? Cosmetics?"

Dumarest shook his head, wondering why the girl seemed incapable of making individual assessments. A woman would have demanded cosmetics, a man also if he belonged to a culture in which he would normally use them, but surely she must have noticed he wore no paint or powder?

"Are you sure, my lord?" She was eager to please.

"I'm sure." Dumarest added casually, "Are there many guests in the house?"

"My lord?"

"It's possible I know one of them." The hint was too vague and she made no response. "A friend of mine," he explained. "A tall man wearing a scarlet robe." Description enough for a cyber and to be too detailed would be to indulge in guesswork. Even as it was not all cybers were tall. "Well?"

"I'm not sure, my lord." Recollection was beyond her, and yesterday was an eternity away. Or else she had been ordered to act the simpleton. "But you'll see them all soon," she said brightly. "At the banquet. My lady sent me to warn you it commences in an hour's time."

Charisse sat at the head of the board, regal in her splendor hair and throat alive with scintillant gems, a queen dispensing hospitality, the guests her devoted subjects, but Dumarest knew there was method in her generosity. The others at the table were buyers from various worlds come to purchase stock or place their needs for specialized forms. Agents of both sexes acted for wealthy consortiums or enlightened rulers, for supply houses or communities wanting to ease life on hostile planets.

Charisse had introduced them with a casual gesture.

"Earl, meet some friends of mine. Enrice, Cleo, Krantz—all of you, meet Earl Dumarest."

That had been before they had taken their places, time for casual drinks and conversation and less casual study. All seemed to be what they claimed; buyers who had waited patiently to get down to business and who now were about to relax over good food and wine.

"Your health, Charisse!" Enrice Helva, old, fat, a little ridiculous with his blouse of puffed and ornamented lace, his trousers of slashed and frilled satin, lifted his glass as he called the toast. "May your genius never wither!"

The wish was shared and for a moment there was silence.

"Charisse may—"

"No, Lunerach." She was firm. "Too many toasts will ruin appetites though I thank you for your good wishes. Now let us eat before we annoy the cook—a good chef is hard to find."

She had found one of the best and Dumarest watched as servants carried in a succession of dishes, each a minor work of art. The tastes matched the display and he helped to ruin castles, farms, boats, ranked armies, birds dressed in golden plumage, beasts formed of sugar and pastry and spices to form perfect miniature zoos. Over fruit and jellies and cakes made of pungent herbs and various flours the talk shifted and swung like a ship in a tormented sea.

"Eighteen," said Ienda Chao. "That's all they could afford, but I ask you! Eighteen when I knew the minimum had to be at least double that. With forty, I told them, you have a chance. With fewer none at all."

"So what happenerd?" Her neighbor cracked a nut and gnawed at the meat with strong, white teeth. "A wipeout?"

"What else? Every last beast was dead within a matter of weeks. They tried to blame me, said I'd bought bad stock, but that was ridiculous and they knew it. They paid the price of greed and ignorance. More stock would have been able to suffer the anticipated losses and left a residue for successful breeding."

"It happens." A woman dressed in somber black reached for a fruit and shredded the peel with glinting nails. "The expert is the last to be listened to. I sometimes wonder if greed robs the intelligence. What do you think, Earl?" Her eyes, darkly ringed with cosmetics, searched his face. "You've sat very quietly—nothing to say?"

"I prefer to listen."

"How nice for your companion—if she too is a good listener." She chuckled at her own jest. "Have you no opinions?"

"None of importance." Dumarest picked up a shard of cake and crumbled it between his fingers. "For one man greed is the desire to obtain more—for another it can be economic necessity."

A man facing him lifted his eyebrows. "Meaning?"

"Nothing, but what you may call greed could be simple lack of funds."

"Farmers!" A woman lower down the table shook her head. "You can't know them as I do, Earl. Always pleading poverty. Offer them good stock and they whine they can't afford the price. Warn them of potential risks and they'll swear you're trying to cheat them. Like Astin I know them too well."

"Especially the male ones, eh, Glenda?" Laughter followed the speaker's comment. "How many deals have you sealed in a barn?"

"As many as you, Corm, but at least I draw the line at cows."

More laughter and Dumarest guessed she had touched on a sore subject—the meat of an old joke. He sat back as the talk continued, uninterested in financial deals, stories of profits earned, of dangers avoided. Charisse noted his detachment.

"We are being discourteous," she said. "What has Dumarest to do with farms and stock? Has none of you any ideas of how to entertain him?"

"I could think of something." The woman in black smiled from where she sat. "Have we anything in common, Earl? Worlds we both know, for example? Pleasures we have both shared?"

"I doubt the first," he said dryly. "I'm not so sure about the second."

"Thank God for a man with a sense of humor," she said. "Charisse, where did you find him? If you ever get around to producing copies of him in your laboratory I'll be your first customer."

"Earl is unique, Linda. I'd like to keep him that way."

"I can't blame you." Her nails glinted as she reached for another fruit, a gleam which attracted his attention, focused his eyes. "You like them?" She extended her hands to show the metal implants. "I've found them useful at times."

"A harlot's trick," sneered Glenda. "You advertise yourself, my dear."

"You have no need, Glenda." The sneer was returned. "Everyone knows your weakness—or is it your depravity?"

"Bitch!"

Dumarest said, loudly, "I was interested in what Armand was trying to achieve. Sayer told me about it."

"The teleths?"

"No, why he developed them."

"The Original Man." Charisse held up a hand and a servant came to fill her glass with wine. A gesture and others attended to the guests. "Armand was certain we had devolved from a higher life form," she explained. "He worked on the theory that nature does not produce organs just to let them wither. The vermiform appendix, the pineal gland—are you with me?"

"If the appendix were functional we could live on cellulose," said Dumarest. He added, "There have been times when I would have found that most convenient."

"To live on grass?" Lina Ynya was quick with her comment. "Earl, you surpise me. Do you really mean that?"

"If you'd ever gone hungry on a world covered with bushes and grass you'd know I mean it. But the pineal gland?"

"Something left over like the appendix," said Charisse. "Some say it's the vestigial remains of a third eye. Can you imagine what it would be like to have three eyes? Think of the advantage you'd have over binocular vision."

"Would there be any?" Corm burped and hastily drank some wine. "The spice," he complained. "Your chef is too heavy with the spice. But to get back to eyes, Charisse, what advantage would a third one give?"

"Maybe it enabled its owner to see into the ultraviolet," suggested Krantz. He was big, solid, his head matted with a grizzle of hair. He added, frowning, "But would that really be an advantage? Of course, if the lens could be adjusted we'd have telescopic vision. That would be an aid to anyone."

"Couldn't you develop something like that yourself, Charisse?" said Vayne. "Build a superbeing. It could be fun?"

"Now you're talking about genetic manipulation," protested Glenda. "Armand was concerned with natural devolution. If we have devolved then from what?"

"Speculation." Astin signaled for more wine. "I've heard such fantasies before. The proposition that we are the products of a genetic engineer—a creature who took beasts and fashioned them into men. In the light of Charisse's achievements is that such an impossible conception? Of course it gives rise to further speculation—who and what was this supposed manipulator? Where did it come from and what happened to it? Did we, Mankind, get out of hand and turn against our creator?" He drank and chuckled at the conception. "Now where have I heard that before?"

In legends, the stuff in which Boulaye had delved, in which Armand Chetame had dealt. A myth Charisse had casually mentioned—or had it been casual? Dumarest glanced at her where she sat, face misted with winking gleams, hair a mass of supporting stars. If bored she gave no sign of it but he had the impression that, like a puppet master, she was manipulating them all.

Now she said, "We have talked enough about my specialty for a while. Let us change the subject. As I recall, Ienda, you mentioned a game before dinner."

"I did?" Ienda had a smooth, pleasant face which now crinkled in thought. "Was it something to do with testing mental ability?"

"Logic. You said it was an exercise in logic which showed how wrong logic can be."

"I remember! It's a game I used to play as a child. No matter what was proposed the answer was always the same. One arrived at by logical deduction."

Lunerarch spoke for the first time since his attempt to propose a toast. "An example, my dear? Can you give us an example?"

"Let me think." She did so, frowning. "Take a beehive. A hive is a dwelling for a number of separate units. In order to live in close proximity units must live in a building. Therefore a hive is a building. A building is a house. You see?" Her triumph was short-lived. "Oh! I didn't give the key word. It was 'house,' of course."

"And everything comes back to house?" Astin was dubious. "Let me see, now. No matter what I say, what word I give you, it all comes to the same, right?"

"Yes."

"Then I'll give you a word. Fish."

"Fish?"

"That's right." He beamed his victory. "You want to back out?"

"No, but I'll take a wager. Even money I don't fail?" She smiled as he nodded. "Three hundred?" Her smile grew wider as, again, he agreed. "Fish? Let me think for a moment. Yes, I have it. A fish has silver scales. A silver-scaled fish is a silverfish. A silverfish lives in a house. Anything which lives in a house is a part of that house. Therefore a fish is a house."

"That's cheating." Enrice Heva shook his head in mock disapproval. "Ienda, you disappoint me."

"It isn't cheating, it's logic," she said. "Can I help it if logic itself is a cheat?"

"A cheat?" The woman in black gave a throaty chuckle. "Not a house?"

"Linda, be charitable, it's only a game."

"So you won't expect to be paid," said Astin. "The bet was a part of the game too."

"Everything is a game. Life, the universe, all a game." Vayne blinked as he reached for his goblet and it toppled beneath his hand. Ruby wine stained the cloth, sent little runnels between the scattered dishes. "How did that happen?"

"Bad coordination," said Charisse. A servant came to swab up the spilled wine at her signal. "You misjudged time, distance and application."

Which, thought Dumarest, was a neat way of telling a man he was drunk.

Time passed, servants coming to clear the table of all but the decanters, the glasses, the bowls of nuts and tiny biscuits, the morsels which cleansed the mouth of present flavors with a diversity of their own. Things to punctuate the conversation as the entertainment divided the topics.

"Clever!" Linda clapped with languid enjoyment as a trio of jugglers made their exit from the hall. "But I think I liked the singer more."

He had been tall and darkly handsome with a voice as clear as a bell and a tonal range which caused it to throb like an organ to rise shrilling as a bird. A virtuoso followed by a dancer with a body of lithe grace, a teller of yarns of questionable taste, a harpist, a girl who played a flute.

Items forgotten as soon as enjoyed as were the wine, the morsels. Dumarest selected one, crushed it between his teeth and felt his mouth fill with a blend of flowers and bees. Another yielded the fragrance of the sea. A third burned with searing spice.

A gamble taken and lost, the forfeit a gulp of cooling wine.

Others paid the price without having lost the game but, he noted, Charisse remained in icy aloofness, her seat at the head of the table the position of control. Even as he watched he saw her signal to one of the servants, a gesture which resulted in the girl moving from one to the other with a tray of small glasses each filled with a lambent fluid.

Taking one Astin lifted it with a mocking smile.

"To the death of pleasure," he said carefully. "To the magic of science!"

Linda, her words more slurred, echoed the sentiment. Drinking, she sat, eyes closed, the empty glass in her hand; then, shuddering, she smiled.

"You bitch," she said clearly. "You laced the medicine with something horrible. If it weren't too late I'd rather have stayed tipsy."

"Instead of which you are sober, my dear," leered fat old Enrice Heva. "And forgetful too, I hope?"

"My door will be unlocked," she retorted. "But if the wrong man comes through he'll regret it."

"And the right one, my dear?"

"He'll know." Her eyes rested on Dumarest. "If he doesn't he will before long."

An invitation openly and unmistakably extended—was she as sober as she seemed? Was any of them? Drunkenness could stem from other sources than alcohol and what had been added to the morsels, dusted on the nuts and biscuits?

"Earl?" Charisse leaned forward in her chair. "You haven' drunk the restorative."

He didn't need it and didn't intend drinking it but it wa better to pretend than refuse. He masked the glass in hi hand, setting it untouched down among others still full. If the girl holding the tray noticed the deception she made no sign.

"Now," said Charisse. "Let us play another game, a seriou one this time. I want you to specify the perfect man."

"Armand's ideal," said Astin. "Well, why not? Do yo want me to begin? We need strength, stamina, an efficient er ergy to food ratio, good sensory apparatus, deft manipulativ ability, a wide temperature tolerance, protection and offensiv weaponry and—" He frowned. "Have I left anything out?"

"I don't think so but I may remember something."

"A man," said Krantz. "We are talking about a man."

"Novaman," said Astin. "The new man. How should he b designed? For strength we need powerful muscles which i turn calls for massive bones for anchorage. But heavy bon show a diminishing return in relation to agility and massi bulk needs a higher intake of food to maintain efficienc There has to be an optimum balance."

"No flying," said Vayne. "A strong bone structure rul that out—the weight factor is against it. Swimming, climbin easy mobility can all be gained by using accepted patterns. But there has to be something more than an extra efficient man. A new method of energy intake, for example. And, now that I think about it, I'm not too sure about the wings. Flying men are common in legend." He appealed to his hostess. "Charisse—can it be done?"

"Efficiently? No."

"The bone weight?"

"Is, as you say, against it. In any case it would restrict our creature to a limited environment. Earl?"

He said, "I'm not a genetic engineer."

"Neither are your companions but they do not hesitate to give their views. Surely you, with your knowledge and experience of various worlds, have some ideas of your own?"

"I mentioned one."

"An active appendix. Nothing else?"

"A fighter would naturally think of a better fighter as superior," said Linda. "A lover someone with better abilities than his own." She ran the tip of her tongue over her lower lip. Pouting, it glistened with the applied moisture. "Which are you, Earl? A fighter? A lover? A blend of both?"

"He'd need to be a hero to take on a strumpet like you." Enrice Heva, smarting at her rejection, took a belated revenge. "Do what you like with your door, Linda, I'll gamble a thousand to one he'll not try to open it."

"Shut your mouth," she said with cold venom. "Insult me again and you'll regret it."

"Enough!" Charisse slammed her hand down hard on the table. "This bickering gains nothing. Now, Earl, give us your idea of the perfect being."

"For the answer to that all you need to do is talk to a monk."

"The Church?" He had surprised her. "What could those beggars know of life? They skulk and preach the doctrine of Universal Brotherhood and enjoy their privation. What do they know of life?"

"The bad side."

"Earl?"

"They've seen it all." Dumarest picked up his glass and tilted it so the ruby wine it contained trembled on the verge of spilling. "The pain and hunger and sacrifice," he said. "The frustration and thwarted desires and the desperation." A

111

drop of wine fell from the glass to splash on the table. "And, the most terrible of all, the death of hope."

"And?"

"They would tell you to create a being who is kind. One who is gentle. A creature who has thought and concern for others. Something which has the imagination to realize the results of its actions. The shape is unimportant. The agility, the strength of body and bone, the stamina, the ability to run or swim or fly. All it would need is tolerance. It's most important organ a heart."

The woman in black said gently, "But Earl, how long would such a creature last?"

"In the jungles we have created? Not long." Dumarest sent more wine to follow the initial drop, a thin stream of metaphorical blood which splashed to run writhing streams. A theatrical gesture which held their attention, their eyes. "If we were created by some alien genetic engineer as you have speculated then, if it intended to fashion monsters, it has done well." The rest of the wine gushed to be spread by the falling glass. "Think of what you do," he said. "Of what you permit others to do. Then look into a mirror and see the shape of a beast."

You'll see intelligence and understanding take the essence of life and create monsters and freaks and cripples doomed to misery, they and their children after them in an endless dynasty of pain. In the wine he could see the dim shapes of the teleths—pathetic beings made for use as toys. The dogs the thing he had fought, the things he had seen. Wine and shattered glass spattered from beneath the hand he slamme on the table.

"Earl!" Charisse had risen, was leaning toward him, one hand lifted to signal. "Earl—are you ill?"

"No." He took a deep, shuddering breath, followed it with another. The sudden rage subsided, the blackness edging his vision receding so he could see the startled faces of his fellow guests. "A momentary indisposition," he said, and twisted his lips into a smile. "If any are offended I apologize." He lightened his tone. "The wine is stronger than I thought."

A weak excuse but one they accepted. It had been a mistake not to have drunk the restorative. Whatever was in must have neutralized the compounds they had been fed Drugs to induce hostility, overt sexuality, vulgar humor.

112

game, he realized. Charisse was triggering emotions to the surface for her inspection. Why had she guided the talk to a superior man?

Linda said, "You've answered my question, Earl. A fighter without a doubt. I saw murder in your face just then."

"Does not every lover kill a little?" Astin was cynical. "Charisse, your entertainment grows stronger each time we meet. One day, perhaps, it will get too strong."

But not while she had guards at her call. Dumarest looked at his palm, the wine staining it, the shallow gash at the base of one finger. Small payment for a stupid act—he'd been luckier than he deserved.

Charisse said, "We have talked about a superior being and yet never have we mentioned how such a creature is to be tested. Do we all agree that, in the final essence, the ability to survive is all-important?"

Vayne said, "Can there be any doubt?"

"None, but I wanted you to admit it. As I want you now to know that I have created just such a creature." She stilled the storm of comment. "No, later you may see it, but not now. But I am in the mood for a wager. You will agree that I know my trade? That if I say the thing I have fashioned is as good as can be devised I can be trusted to know what I'm talking about?"

Astin said, "Your point, Charisse?"

"If you so agree you will not hesitate to back it to win. Agreed?"

"The terms?"

"If it wins I will supply copies at basic cost. If it fails I will take your cash. Two thousand each, I think, would be fair. Earl—"

He said flatly, "No."

"You refuse?"

"To fight, yes."

"A pity. Must I remind you that you are in my debt?"

"For the cost of a passage. I admit it."

"For your life, Earl." She paused then repeated. "For your life. A debt now to be cleared. Fight my creature and, if you win, you owe me nothing."

And he would gain no more than he had. If he was forced to entertain then he would demand his fee. She frowned as he told her what it was.

"The library? You want access to the library?"

"To that and to Armand's personal files. The material he collected in his investigation into the old legends." As she nodded he said sharply, "You agree?"

"Of course."

He felt himself relax, tension leaving him as if it were water pouring from an open faucet. All that remained now was to fight, to win, to gain the secret he had come to find and to be on his way.

Chapter Nine

The contest was to be at noon, held in an open space before one of the barrack-like buildings. An area of some hundred yards square, ringed by a high hedge of close-set thorns, their spines masked with a profusion of small, purple blooms.

"An exercise yard," explained Dino Sayer. "We use it to allow specimens to demonstrate their mobility."

Their agility, grace, aptitudes and, now, the ability to kill. Dumarest looked at the building, the door set in the side facing him, closed now, but soon to open. The roof was a hundred feet above the ground, the wall sheer, the expanse unbroken aside from the door. At points along the edge he saw rounded blobs which could have been the heads of watching men.

"I don't like this," said the old man. "Testing a new product is one thing, but we usually set them against other beasts or those of their own kind. This is nothing but murder."

"You think it will win?"

The man's silence was answer enough. Dumarest looked again at the building, the hedge, the ground on which he stood. Lush grass cropped short made a mantle over soft loam. The sun, at zenith, stared like a bloodshot eye from the sky.

"How long must we wait?" Enrice Heva was impatient. "Why the delay?"

"Does it matter?" Linda Ynya snapped her irritation. She looked worn, haggard, her face raddled beneath the paint. Like the others she stood in a gallery which ran along one side of the square; a raised platform set beyond the hedge and shielded by a canopy. She added, "Don't worry, Enrice, you'll have your fun. Earl can't escape."

That conviction was shared by them all. Astin turned as Charisse joined her guests. She wore a gown of glinting ruby; metal threads catching and reflecting the sunlight so that she stood as if wreathed in flame.

Looking at her, Ienda Chao said, "Earl is still dressed and armed. Surely he should be naked if the contest is to be fair?"

"An animal has its hide," said Linda quickly. "Its pelt and claws and fangs."

"Natural attributes." Vayne pointed out. "Ienda has a point. Even if he retains his clothing he should yield the knife."

"Let him keep it," said Krantz. "If the creature is truly superior what difference will it make?"

That comment ended the discussion. At Charisse's command Sayer moved toward the building, the door it contained, turning once to look at Dumarest then striding ahead, a man not liking what he did but one who would do it just the same. Krantz and Linda had been better allies though their motives could be less than altruistic. But why had Charisse allowed him to keep the knife? Of them all she knew how well he could use it.

Did she want her creation to win?

A thought considered and dismissed as Dumarest again searched the area. The hedge was thick, growing low, the spaces at the base few and too small to allow of passage. A barrier a dozen feet high, the spines a host of knives to rip and tear at flesh which came too close. The platform itself was beyond reach—the only obvious route to freedom lay through the door.

The panel opened as he watched to reveal a shadowed

darkness in which something moved. A shape loped forward to stand in the crimson light of the sun.

"God!" said someone from the platform. "Dear, God!"

A woman's voice, but Dumarest couldn't tell which. There was no time to look, no time for anything but to study the creature before him. The creation from the laboratories which Charisse had claimed to be a superior man.

She had lied—he looked at a woman.

Like himself she was dressed in neutral gray, fabric which covered her body but there was no mistaking the thrust of breasts, the swell of hips and thighs. A body designed for breeding, for the first necessity of any superior life form was the ability to reproduce. The frame was massive and he guessed genetic science had developed hollow bones for greater muscle anchorage without added weight. The skin was a deep brown, the eyes widely spaced and deep-set beneath thrusting brows. The forehead was high, curved, surmounted by a mane of ebon hair. The mouth showed the white gleam of pointed incisors—feline teeth which could stab and rip like knives. The hands were large, the fingers equipped with retractable claws.

A blend of woman and cat, she stood eight feet tall, loping toward him intent on his death.

Dumarest turned and ran, turning again to duck beneath a reaching hand, to be sent sprawling as a foot hammered at his side. A blow which numbed, then repeated to rip sod from the ground and send it flying high and far to one side. Speed which would have killed had it been backed with experience. Which would kill if he allowed it time.

Again he ran, seeing the wall of the building rise before him, the closed door. Behind its grill he saw eyes, the glint of metal, saw too the shadow darkening the steel. A warning he obeyed just in time, throwing himself to one side as the woman slammed into the panel, wood shredding beneath the rake of her nails.

The impetuous anger of youth and she had to be young. Something patterned in the laboratory and forced to speeded maturity with the aid of slowtime. Fed with artificial concentrates, exercised by machines, the body developed at the expense of the mind. An idiot, unable as yet to talk, to think, to understand. A reactive construct which had been programmed to destroy.

Against it his knife was useless.

She was too fast, too well-protected. Even if he blinded an eye it would do nothing to slow her. Unlike the mannek she had been designed for efficiency and not for display. The pain level must be high, nerves and tendons duplicated, survival responses built into the very fabric of her being. The common attributes of any female were in her developed to the ultimate.

Yet there had to be weaknesses.

He dodged again, staying beyond reach of the clawed hands, moving with trained response while his mind assessed the situation. He could cut and slash and wound but each of her hands held five knives against his one. She was as fast as he was. Taller than he. Stronger. His only advantage lay in his experience—the cunning developed over the years.

And she was a woman and a child.

He ran, stooping as he ran, to straighten with the weight of his knife in his hand. Nine inches of honed and tempered steel blazed like a crimson icicle as he lifted the polished blade to catch and reflect the sunlight. A flashing glitter vanished to reappear again as he maneuvered the weapon. Darting rays caught the woman across the eyes, making her blink, making her lift shielding hands, causing her to halt, to back a little from the unknown and therefore potentially dangerous brightness.

But the childish mind was entranced even as the mature body reacted to programmed caution.

Dumarest edged to one side, boots soundless on the sward, knife lifted, reflected brightness aimed at the face, the eyes. He backed and she followed, one hand reaching for the knife. He backed even more then stepped quickly around her so that her back was toward the hedge opposite to that holding the platform.

"Here!" he said. "Catch!"

Crimson gleamed as he threw the knife.

It rose high, spinning, a glittering wheel which spun up and toward the hedge. A thing of magic which she followed with her eyes, hands lifting to snatch it from the air, falling short as it soared above the thorns. She turned to face it, stepping forward—and Dumarest moved.

He ran forward, leaping high, one boot landing on the swollen curve of her buttocks, using it as a foothold to leap again, jumping high as he used the broad shoulders as a platform. The leap carried him after the knife, the hedge passing beneath him, thorns rasping at his clothing as he fell, hands clamped protectively over his eyes.

He landed on soft dirt, legs folding to cushion the shock, hands falling as his eyes searched for the knife. It rested a dozen feet away, half sunken in the loam, and he snatched it up, running as he heard shouts from behind, Charisse's sharp order.

"Stop him! Use the stunner!"

Another voice, thin with distance. "My lady—it doesn't work!"

An unsuspected bonus—the thing planted in his temple had been more than a vehicle for the drugs which had dulled his mind.

"Try again!" she ordered and then, as Dumarest continued to run, "Stop, Earl—or I'll loose the dogs!"

He heard the snuffle and tensed, lying in the gloom of the hut, concentrating on simple orders. Outside the teleths moved in an apparently random pattern, blocking the door, crossing the paths, ruining what scent he may have left with their own, pungent odors. A score of them milling to halt and watch with their large, staring eyes. The snuffling faded and in the shadows Dumarest relaxed.

He was hot, his body sticky with perspiration beneath his clothing, the garments themselves ripped and scratched by thorns and hooked leaves, spines and barbed protrusions. His hands were webs of scratches, his hair matted, his boots slimed. For an eternity, it seemed, he had run and dodged and wended his way through an elaborate maze. Hiding from the rafts and men sent to search for him, the dogs, the loping felines many of which he had left in puddles of blood and fur. A path which had led him to the village of the teleths was the only safety he could hope to find.

Through the low arch of the door he could see a small patch of darkening sky. Already it blazed with a scatter of stars heralding the night as the last rays of crimson bid farewell to the day. Soon it would be dark and the grounds filled with the dogs newly commanded to kill. Before then he must be on his way.

Cautiously he moved to the opening and saw the assembled

119

shapes outside. There were too many to be normal and he concentrated on watching as small groups moved away to wander aimlessly about the paths, the sown plots of ground. A normal scene for any who might be watching and, later, unless bathed in the glow of a searchlight, he might pass as one of the teleths. Their radiated body heat, at least, would mask his own as their scent baffled the dogs.

The stars shone brighter then dulled as a scud of cloud came to blur their images, clouds which thickened to shed a drizzling rain. It drummed on his head as Dumarest left the shelter, washed the blood from his scratches, the dirt from flesh and clothing. The downpour sent the teleths into shelter from which he drove them with savage, mental commands. Humped, miserable, they shuffled with himself among them toward the house.

It was farther than he remembered, the space between interspersed with compounds, stockades, feeding plots, pools. Areas were divided by spined barriers, some set with gates, others with elaborate stiles. The obstructions broke the shielding knot of teleths and sent them wandering in individual confusion. This was a gain rather than a loss and one achieved without his direction.

From somewhere he heard the belling of a hound.

It came again, closer, a deep-toned baying from the west. Another dog or the first signaling its new position to the leader of the pack? One who could have found a teleth and was marking the position. The creatures wouldn't be harmed—only he stood in danger.

A pool glinted before him and Dumarest plunged into it, risking what it might contain in an attempt to negate his scent. The far bank held a matted moss which moved as he gripped it, tendrils rising from the seemingly harmless vegetation to wind around his arms, his legs, his throat. Strands which tightened and pulled him back into the water. Ropes of living tissue studded with mouths seeking his blood.

He felt the stink and tore free an arm to rip the tendrils from his throat. Others replaced them and he felt the blood drum in his ears as they closed in a strangling noose. He strained, reaching for his knife, lifting it from his boot to send the edge against the living ropes. A slash and they had parted, ends falling as he pulled them from his neck. Pearls of blood showed dark in the growing starlight as the rain clouds thinned as they drifted to the south. More cuts and he was free, stepping over the matted fronds to firm ground.

He paused as again he heard the belling of a hound. A hedge stood before him, a barrier set with a flight of wooden steps leading to a small platform, more steps the other side. As he watched he heard the rasp of claws, saw the stairs quiver as something mounted the far side. He ran forward, crouching against the base of the hedge as a dog jumped down and loped toward the pool.

It was one of the pack he had seen and, at close quarters, was even more forbidding than when seen from the safety of a raft. It halted, sniffing, nose rising as it looked around. Before it, close to the matted growth at the edge of the pool, slashed tendrils twitched like blind and severed worms. This was sure evidence of recent intrusion and Dumarest knew the dog had recognized it as such. As the head lifted to bay a signal to the pack he lunged forward, the knife extended in his hand.

As the beast turned, the knife plunged deep into the corded throat.

A calculated stab which cut the main arteries and sent blood to drown the bay, the warning barks. The wound would kill, had killed, but even though as good as dead the beast retained energy, the ingrained compulsion to kill. It snarled, teeth gleaming white, reddening as blood sprayed from its muzzle. A fountain preceded the final attack, the dog's jaws opening, closing on Dumarest's lifted forearm, clamping on the sleeve, the mesh it contained, the flesh and bone within.

Trapped by the grip, Dumarest fell back beneath the dying weight, lay still as he heard a man calling from the platform.

"Chando? Where are you, boy?" He held a flashlight and shone its beam over the area. It settled on the dog, the man beneath. "God! Hold, boy! Hold!"

Dumarest tensed as boots rattled down the stairs. His left forearm was still clamped between the jaws now locked in death, his right hand holding the knife pressed between the beast and his stomach. If the man had seen the blood he must imagine it came from the victim and not the dog. As he came closer Dumarest groaned.

"Chando!" The voice held the snap of command. "Up, boy! Up!"

"He's got me," said Dumarest weakly. "Help me. Help."

"Just stay where you are, mister." The man's voice held the confidence of one backed by an army. "A word from me and Chando will rip out your throat. Now, boy, that's enough. Up, I tell you. Up!"

Dumarest heaved, the dog moving a little, a semblance of life in the shadows, the drifting glare of the flashlight; a moment of confusion in which he managed to free his knife, to ease his legs. The movement of his trapped arm made it seem as if the dog were lifting its head.

"That's better!" The man echoed his satisfaction at the apparent obedience. "You—" He broke off as he saw the throat, the stained teeth. In the beam of the flashlight the dog's eyes were dull and lifeless gems. "Dead," he said blankly. "Dead—but how?"

"Help me." Dumarest moaned as if in pain. The animal's blood masked his face, gave him the appearance of injury, of a throat torn by fangs. "Please, help me."

"Like hell," snapped the guard. "You bastard! You killed Chando."

The man loved his charges and was eager for revenge. Dumarest reared as he snatched at the whistle hanging from his neck, knowing that one blast would bring the pack racing to bring him down. As it rose to the lips he lifted his hand, the knife a blur as it left his fingers, the pommel making a dull, wooden sound as it slammed against the guard's temple. As he slumped Dumarest tore his arm free of the clamping jaws and ran to recover the weapon. He froze as a voice came from lower down the hedge.

"Levie? Is that you?"

Another guard patroled the area, his voice casual above the rasp of booted feet on the graveled path. Dumarest found the flashlight and killed the beam. From where he lay sprawled on the ground its owner made small, burbling noises which died as he was turned over on his side.

"Levie?" The footsteps halted on the far side of the hedge. "Is that you in there?"

Silence would answer his question but could arouse suspicion. Dumarest coughed, made grunting noises, stamped heavily on the stairs and turned on the flashlight as he reached the platform. In its light a small, round-faced man peered upward, lifting a shielding hand as the beam focused on his eyes.

"Be careful with that thing," he snapped. "You want to blind me?" His voice rose as the dim shape behind the light came closer. "Levie! What the hell—"

He sagged as stiffened fingers thrust like blunted spears into the major nerves of his throat, a blow which stunned but did not kill. Before he reached the ground Dumarest was running toward the house which lifted its bizarre silhouette against the sky.

Linda Ynya was bored. The party had turned sour and despite the money she had won at cards, she felt irritable and, somehow, cheated. It was Charisse's fault, of course; she had refused to make the matter clear, leaving them to argue. Had Dumarest won or had he lost? He hadn't killed the creature but neither had he been killed. Did his escape prove he was the more superior or not? A point which Astin even now was trying to determine.

"Dumarest defeated the objective of the creature which was to kill him," he insisted. "So the thing failed to do what it intended."

"Which means nothing." Vayne slopped wine into a glass, sipped, made a grimace as if he found it sour. "Or are you saying cowardice is a mark of valor?"

"Cowardice has nothing to do with it." Krantz was impatient. "The man fought and escaped with his life. More than that; he was uninjured and so able to fight again. The point you all overlook is that he used his brains. If we accept intelligence as being superior to ignorance then the decision is plain. Dumarest won."

This was what Charisse wanted them to accept so she could take their money and give nothing in return. Was Krantz in her pay? Had she promised him some advantage for having helped Dumarest? It had been his suggestion that the knife should be permitted—but she had argued against stripping him and she had received nothing. A question of fairness, she thought, or had it been more than that? A disinclination to see him made a helpless victim or her own feelings reflected in her defense. To be naked was to be helpless in more ways than one.

"My dear?" Enrice Heva was at her side. "It seems we bore you. Some wine?"

She shook her head.

"Another diversion, perhaps?" His leer left no doubt as to his meaning. "If you are agreeable I would be happy to cooperate."

"You've had my answer to that," she snapped. "I don't want to repeat it. If you are so hungry for a bedmate try Cleo. Or Glenda—I understand she has a taste for perversion. You should amuse her." She smiled with undiluted malice. "Or disappoint her—even she needs a man."

"Bitch!"

"Yes?" She met his eyes. "And?"

He backed away, scowling, knowing better than to insult her further. A coward—would he have dared to face one of Charisse's creatures? Would she? An empty question, she knew the answer too well, but Dumarest had and she wondered why. A matter of a debt, she'd gathered, that and a promise given. How gratifying it must be to have power over such a man.

A servant offered wine and she waved it aside leaning back in her chair to study the others. Ienda Chao and Lunerarch were absent and it took no genius to know where they were and what they were doing. Glenda would probably sleep with Corm or, this time, it could be Astin. Cleo—what the hell did it matter who slept with whom?

"A draw," said Krantz. "The result can only be a draw. They met, neither was hurt, the contest was ended."

"That proves the lack of superiority of Charisse's creation." Enrice, smarting at her rejection, found refuge in taking a stand in the argument. "So the man won."

"Which means you are happy to see Charisse collect." Vayne took another sip of wine. "I don't feel so generous."

"You think she will agree to supply copies as promised?"

"No, which is why we had better all agree with Krantz. If the result is a draw then no one has to lose." Vayne looked at Linda as she rose. "Leaving us so soon?"

"I'm tired. I'm going to bed."

"Alone?"

She heard their laughter as she climbed the stairs.

Her room was set high in the building, a large chamber softly decorated, fitted with all a person could need. The bed was wide and soft and covered with a fabric of rich material adorned with arabesques of gold set against a field of black. A servant had placed a decanter of wine beside it together with a pair of glasses, a subtle comment by her hostess which she chose to ignore. Charisse could be generous but always with reason, and her order, this time, had been large. A score of mutated cattle together with two breeding pairs of dogs, some birds genetically engineered to consume a particular species of troublesome insect and the eggs of serpents able to live on dust, sun and apparently little else.

Now, work done, she could afford to relax and estimate her profit.

She could think, too, of the spectacle she had seen.

Krantz had been wrong—if there had been a winner it had to be Dumarest but she would go along with his decision for the sake of peace. In any case she had no use for a copy of the monster no matter what the cost and, she remembered, Charisse had left it deliberately vague. But of one thing she had no doubt; if Dumarest could be persuaded to fight in an arena he would make a fortune.

She poured wine and stood sipping wondering why she had left the others so early. Tiredness had been an excuse induced by boredom but there had to be more than that. An impatience to leave, perhaps; the Chetame Laboratory held little inducement to linger once business had been done.

A touch of chill caused her to shiver and she turned, staring at the window, frowning when she saw it open. The fault of some careless servant who would have paid for it had she been back home. While the days on Kuldip were warm, the nights were cold, the more so after the early rain. And the wind, blowing toward her room, brought added discomfort.

Setting down the glass, she moved toward the open pane, reaching forward to catch the edge of the outward-swung window, pausing to stare outside. The cloud had thickened and the rain had returned driving toward her in vagrant showers driven by equally vagrant winds. A bad night to be in the open, a worse one when hunted, and she shivered at the distant baying of a hound. God help Dumarest if the animals should catch him.

God help Charisse if they did not.

She touched the glazed panel and pulled it toward her then froze as she saw the broken spot at the edge near the catch, the glass shattered to form an opening ringed with jagged shards—evidence she recognized immediately for what it had to be.

Somehow, incredibly, Dumarest had managed to elude the guards, to climb the wall and to break a hole in the window to gain entry into her room. She had returned too soon for him to have closed it and drawn the curtains. She wondered what he would have done had she screamed. She had no doubt of what would have happened had she been Charisse.

Chapter Ten

He stepped from the bathroom where he had to be and she sucked in her breath at the sight of the blood masking his face. The blood was not wholly his own but some had oozed from lacerations on his scalp, and the hand which held the knife poised to throw was bruised, the nails stained with ugly purple, rimmed with fresh carmine.

"You're safe," she said quickly. "I won't scream. I'm long past the age when a man in my bedroom is a cause of fear." He failed to appreciate the humor, and she regretted having made the comment. "You're hurt. Bleeding. Strip and get under the shower." As he hesitated she added, "I won't betray you. I give you my word on that."

One he felt she would keep and he remembered her support at the contest, her attitude at the banquet. She had no love for the owner of the laboratories. And there was an indefinable something which he had known before: an attitude, a concern, a betraying tenderness even though masked by a brusque efficiency. As the water drummed on his head to lave his body with paling streams of carmine, she washed his clothing free of dirt, pursing her lips as she saw the damage.

"What happened out there, Earl? Did you have an argu-

127

ment with tigers? Some of Charisse's pets? And the dogs—did you tangle with them?"

"One. It was enough."

"Is that how you got that arm? You'd better let me take a look at it."

She touched it gently as he stepped from the drier, frowning as she examined the ugly bruises, the mangled skin. Even though dying, the beast had summoned strength enough to have severed the limb had it not been for the protective mesh.

"It's cracked." Her fingers dug deeper. "I'm no doctor but I've worked with animals long enough to have picked up some knowledge. Move your fingers." She grunted her satisfaction as he obeyed. "You were lucky. How the hell did you manage to climb that wall?"

Because, she knew, he'd had no choice. No way of avoiding the pain, the danger, the risk of being spotted, of falling. Now she understood the condition of his hand, the bruises and blood rimmed beneath the nails. The knife would have helped; rammed into cracks, it would have provided holds, but the rest had stemmed from raw courage and determination.

"Here." She handed him a glass of wine, ignoring his nakedness as she ripped fabric into strips to bandage his arm. "What made you pick this room? Luck?"

That and the carvings which alone had made the climb possible. They had led him to the window and his failing strength had left no choice.

As she finished the bandage Linda said quietly, "I suppose you intend killing her now. I can't blame you for wanting that, but, Earl, be careful."

"Guards?"

"If I was Charisse I'd be surrounded with them and I'd have a laser in each hand." She frowned at his untouched wine. "Get that down—it'll do you good."

"I can manage without it."

And what it could contain. She smiled, guessing his thoughts, and reaching for the glass swallowed its contents. Proof only that she had introduced nothing lethal into the wine.

As she set down the glass she said, "Earl, I'm leaving to

morrow. I've a chartered vessel and it'll leave as soon as loading is complete. There's room if you want to come along."

"To where?"

"Souchong. I'm delivering there." Her fingers lingered on the bandage. "Just think about it. Help yourself to wine while I get your clothes."

They were damp but clean and he dressed, ignoring the pain from wrenched muscles, the throb of the cracked bone in his forearm.

As he slipped the knife into his boot she said, "Well? Have you decided? Will you ride with me?" Without waiting for a reply she added, quickly, "No strings. No demands. You can pay if you can afford it or work as a handler if you're broke. I want nothing you're not willing to give. It's just that I hate to see a good man wasted. God knows there are few enough of them."

And few women who would offer help as unhesitatingly as she had. Dumarest stepped toward her, halted, lifted his hands to touch her cheeks, the palms resting lightly against her ears as, gently, with no trace of physical passion, he kissed her lips.

"Earl!"

"You have my gratitude," he said. "Now increase my debt by telling me where to find Charisse."

The place was filled with murmurs, soft susurrations which hung like ghosts in the air; words uttered and relayed to be amplified and distorted by corners and angles and long galleries of wood carved into a multitude of shapes. Beasts and reptiles and things from dark places which seemed to watch with jeweled eyes and move at the edge of vision to freeze when stared at directly. This illusion came from the subdued lighting which left the upper parts of the corridors in shrouded darkness.

Dumarest paused as sound increased to turn into words slurred with intoxication. Enrice Heva, late leaving the party, calling a farewell to Corm. One tinged with bitter envy.

"Sleep well, my friend—if Glenda will let you. And remember, my dear, if he bores you I shall be waiting."

Her reply held the brittle indifference of a wanton.

"Wait on, Enrice. I'll try not to let it worry me."

"Bitch!"

"Old goat!"

"That's enough!" Krantz called a halt to the exchange, his voice breaking to echo in fading, reverberations. "Tomorrow is another day and remember our decision. We all agree—"

The thread of sound died, cut by a closing door, the soft thud of the panel a sonorous drum in the whispering silence. A trick of acoustics turned the stairwell into a whispering gallery. An accident or something created by design. Had Armand Chetame stood at its head listening to the unguarded comments of his guests? Did Charisse?

Dumarest reached it, looking upward, seeing only a spiraling band of pale luminescence. Illumination seemed controlled and directed as was the rest to leave the upper layers in shadow.

He wondered at the absence of guards.

Linda Ynya had warned him against them and he had expected to find them but, as yet, he had roved unchallenged and unmolested along the passages and past the blank faces of endless doors. A search at random; the woman had not been able to tell him where Charisse was to be found.

"I swear it, Earl," she'd said. "I'm only a guest here, remember. A business acquaintance. She could be anywhere or not in the building at all."

A hope he didn't share but if Charisse was absent he could still find the library and, with luck, the secret it might contain.

But, first, the woman.

He moved on, halting as fresh murmurs echoed from the air. Deep masculine tones gave orders barely discernible and Dumarest placed his ear against the paneling to gain clearer definition. A waste, the contact resulted in a total loss and when he backed and cocked his head the murmurs had gone.

Up?

Should he go higher?

He moved on, stepping carefully on the treads, his shoulders prickling as if they were the target for watching eyes. The house was too silent, too deserted, the lighting too odd. There should have been servants if not guards but he had seen no one since leaving Linda's room. Heard nothing but vibrating echoes. Had she given the warning after he'd left?

A gamble he had taken and one he had calculated to win. She had delayed him but for obvious reasons and he ha been willing to spend time in relative safety. She had confessed her attraction, had a chartered vessel ready to leave and was willing to give him passage.

He opened a door and looked at shadows broken by points of brightness; reflections from assembled equipment set on benches. The pressure of a switch brought them into sharper distinction; microscopes, constructs of glass and metal, the blank face of a machine covered in a host of dials. A laboratory? Armand would have worked in the house before the main laboratories had been built. His study? If so the library could be close.

"Raske!" The tone was deep, one he had heard before in a fading whisper, now coming loud and strong from the passage outside. "Take up position here and keep alert. The man is armed and dangerous."

"I know that, sir."

"Don't forget it. Levie has a broken skull and Epel's spitting blood. Both are lucky to be alive. The next time he might kill." A pause then, "I'd better check the doors."

Dumarest had killed the light at the first sound and now he leaned against the panel, fingers searching for the latch. He found it, slid it home as something pressed on the panel from the other side. The guard or his officer—who was unimportant. All that mattered was that he was trapped.

He turned as the pressure ceased to check the room in closer detail. The place was totally dark, no light coming past the edges of the door or from any gap below. A check he made before again switching on the light. A minor risk compared to the noise he would make if he stumbled against one of the glass fabrications. At the far end he saw a window and made his way to it while searching for other doors. One pierced the wall to his left and he opened it to see a multi-drawered cabinet lining one wall. A bench held delicate scales, containers, flasks and other equipment he guessed was used for the measuring and weighing of exact amounts. The cabinet would hold a range of chemical elements and compounds. The flasks to one side in padded racks held acids and other fluids. Everything was clean, free of dust and sparingly bright, but he gained the impression that none of it had been used for some time.

The room had no door, no window and he stepped back to the main room. The window was curtained and he carefully slipped beneath the fabric, opening the pane to check outside. On the ground lights shone, beams flickering from side to side revealing the figures of men and animals. One of the dogs reared, looking upward, small whining sounds coming from its throat.

A moment and Dumarest had closed the window, setting the curtain back into place. A glance had been enough; the wall was sheer, even if he'd been willing to tackle a climb again the lack of holds made it impossible. That and the dogs and men watching from below.

Quietly he paced back to the door and crouched, ear against the panel, listening.

One guard? More?

If so how would they be placed?

He remembered the passage, the doors, the stairs he had climbed. One there, certainly, if the commander knew his job. One at the far end of the corridor—but why one outside this door?

Coincidence?

Or did they know he was inside?

Dumarest straightened, spine prickling with a familiar tension, the deep-rooted primitive warning of danger which he had learned never to ignore. Treading softly he crossed to the inner room and propped the door open with a chair. A switch released a flood of illumination, brilliance which dulled as he wrapped a cloth around the globe. Another chair and some odd items of equipment draped with the curtain from the window made an indistinct shadow against the cabinet. Back at the door he killed the light in the main room, released the catch and lifting a heavy flask he'd taken from the inner room hurled it at the window.

"Sir!" The guard outside called to his officer at the sound of shattering glass. "Sir—he's in here!"

The door slammed wide as he flung his weight against it to stagger into the room. He saw the broken window, the vague silhouette of a man in apparent hiding—and collapsed as Dumarest stepped up behind him and struck at his neck.

"Hold!" The guard at the stairs was armed. He raised the thick barrel of his weapon, the muzzle wavering as he tried to aim. Dumarest raced forward, dived low, rose to send the heel of his palm against the guard's exposed jaw.

The treads of the stairs blurred beneath him as he ran up and away from the men mounting from below.

"Hold!" The deep bellow sent echoes from the walls, the shadowed ceilings. "You can't get away!"

The flight gave on to a landing, a narrow passage running to either side. Without hesitation Dumarest turned left, judging distance and position as he ran. The room he had just left faced east, the window set in the outer wall of the building. But a place so large must have an inner court with windows set around the enclosed space. If he could climb high enough, make his way out on the roof, he would be able to choose where and when he would reenter the building.

A corner and he ducked around it. Twenty paces and a door yielded to the impact of his boot. A peaked dormer window looked out on a slope ending at a gutter, the slope continuing up and back to a flat ledge. Dumarest reached it as light shone from the window he had just left. Levering himself over it, he found a flat area broken with the bulk of spires, gulleys, narrow catwalks, all touched with the fitful light from clouded stars.

The light deluded and robbed the eyes of clear perspective. He bumped into a cowled ventilator shaft, almost tripped over an upraised section of peaked tiles, halted barely in time to prevent stepping into the mouth of a dark cavity.

In it something chittered and scrabbled as it rose.

It was black, touched with the gleam of reflected starlight, chiton gleaming like oiled and polished iron. A creature he had disturbed now rose from its lair. Mandibles rattled like castenets and fitful light revealed gleaming, faceted eyes, a spined and rearing head. A mutated insect ready to rip and tear at the intruder. A beetle-like spider fully seven feet long which attacked with a sudden rush.

Dumarest dropped to his left knee, steel whining as he whipped the blade from his right boot, the edge slicing up and outward to leave a questing antenna lying on the roof. One minor injury quickly followed another as again he slashed to hack at a hooked limb, to roll as mandibles snapped where he had been, to feel space opening beneath him as he halted on the edge of the pit.

It wafted a noisome, acrid stench accompanied by thin stridulations. Sound drowned in the rasp of the creature's legs, the clash of its pincer-like mandibles. Dumarest rose, backing, his left hand extended behind him, searching for the railed catwalk he had spotted earlier. The fingers found metal, closed around the bar as the insect rushed at him. The charge would have knocked him down had it not been for the rail, which sent him hard against it as he ducked to rise under the jaws and send the knife sliding over the armored thorax. The point found a juncture, a softer fold which yielded beneath the thrust of the sharp steel. Dumarest straightened his arm, turning the knife into the metal extension of the spear he'd made of flesh and bone, the insect's own fury driving the blade deep into its body.

The wound sent it backing, head lifted, to turn and dive back into the safety of its lair.

"Dumarest!" The voice came from the window he had left. "Don't move, man. Stay where you are! Just don't move!"

The warning had come too late but told him there could be other dangers. The roof made a good place for mutated creatures to stay and they, in turn, would serve better than human guards. Dumarest climbed over the rail and moved along the catwalk. It ended at a humped bulk and he edged around it, the tip of his knife rasping the stone as he sent it before him. Beyond lay triple ridges supporting flying tresses designed to hold the weight of the chambers below. He moved along them, eyes searching the far side of the courtyard, windows bright in the reflected glow from the light streaming from the dormer. As he watched it darkened as if occluded by a shape.

Someone following him? If so he was wasting his time but if the man wanted to risk his neck it was to Dumarest's advantage. If nothing else he would provide a target for any lurking dangers.

A second courtyard lay behind the first and Dumarest studied it. The small windows running along the edge of the sloped roof were all dark aside from one at the far end. A point of light which he used as a marker, crouching low as he moved along the tiles so as to silhouette anything against it. A slender shaft came into view, passed, was replaced by bulkier ventilator which, in turn, yielded to a humped and rounded mass.

From it came the sudden hum of wings.

Hornets, each as large as a pigeon, rising in a swarm from

their hive as they sensed his nearness, the sweat or heat from his body, the vibration of his tread. Shapes which darted, seeming to hover, to vanish as they darted again, living missiles armed with strings oozing venom.

Dumarest ran, risking a slip, a fall in the desperate need to find a place of relative safety. In the open he was too vulnerable—attacks could be made from all sides—but if he could manage to guard his back he could make a stand. A high coping reared before him, set with alcoves bearing figures of stone. He reached the nearest, tore it from its pedestal, sprang to take its place. As the statue went rolling down the slope of the roof to fall and crash into shards on the ground below, the first of the hornets struck.

It came from above, aiming for the head, missing as Dumarest ducked, to hit the shoulder with the impact of a swung hammer, sting ripping at the plastic, poison staining the bared mesh beneath. The determined and vicious creature died in a mass of pulp as Dumarest threw himself back against the stone. As it fell another joined it, chiton broken, wings shredded beneath the swing of a hand stiffened to form a blunted axe. A weapon paired by the other hand, both weaving, slashing, lifting to stab, to strike, to beat off the mass of droning, spiteful menace.

The coping saved him, that and his speed, the reflexes which allowed him to beat an attack from midair, to knock stings to one side, to send a rain of twitching, broken insects to fall and roll and plummet to the ground. But as fast as they fell others took their place, rising from the hive to wheel, to hover, to dart in with vicious intent. To die in turn beneath the edges of his palms, the thrust of stiffened fingers, to pulp against the shielding stone as he ducked and weaved to dodge and delude.

The battle could only have one end. Already he was aching with fatigue, his left forearm a burning torment. Sweat ran down to sting his eyes and blur his vision, making it even harder to see the attacking hornets. Only their hum saved him at times, the instinct which told him where and when to strike.

And, sometimes, he was too late.

Pain burned on his scalp where a sting had slashed the skin through his hair. Hooked legs had ripped a cheek and his left and was puffed from injected venom. Beneath the ripped

135

plastic his body ached from accumulated bruises and the right side of his throat oozed blood.

Soon a sting would find an eye, the pain ruining his concentration, causing him to flail wildly at the air, leaving himself open to more successful attacks. Within seconds he would be falling, rolling to join the shattered statue, the pulped bodies of the hornets he had sent after it.

Here, in the nighted darkness, on the summit of a roof, he could die.

Would die unless something happened to his advantage. Unless the luck which had saved him so often before served him once again.

A hum and pulp on his swinging hand. Another and a shadow blocking the vision of one eye as his hand stabbed upwards to drive fingers deep into the winged body. More as, like rain, the hornets fell from the sky.

"Dumarest!"

He heard the voice, the sudden glare of light which filled the air with scarlet gossamer from shimmering wings, with red and yellow from mutated bodies.

"Down man! Down!"

An order yelled from beyond the glare of light, one he obeyed, hearing the whine of missiles as he dropped, a hail of darts which blasted the hornets from above where he crouched.

"Hold your breath!"

Vapor this time, a swirling fog which chilled the air and frosted the stone, the tiles, the fallen bodies with a thick, white film. The gas numbed his attackers and sent them to land, swaying on thin, spindle-legs, wings drooping, eyes glassy with disorientation.

"All right, Earl, get aboard."

The raft edged closer, a figure standing before the searchlight, others at the instrument, the controls. As Dumarest rose and stepped forward to grip the rail Dino Sayer came into clear view.

"You were lucky," he said. "Damned lucky. If we'd arrived a couple of minutes later you'd be jelly by now."

Dumarest said nothing, waiting until he was safe, his boots on the deck of the raft, one hand gripping the rail as it lifted up and away from the roof.

"You should have waited," said the old man. "Didn't you

hear the call? The roof's no place to be at anytime especially at night. A man needs to be covered, coated with repellents, armed with a spray before he can venture out. Those hornets will attack anything which comes into their area—and there are other things."

"I met one," said Dumarest. He straightened, easing his muscles, his right hand falling casually toward his right boot, the knife it contained. "Her idea?"

"Charisse? No, Armand set the guards, but she lets them be. No point in clearing them when they've become established and they're no trouble usually." Sayer gave a dry chuckle. "But we don't usually have intruders on the roof." To the driver he snapped, "That's high enough. Back to the station and check in the equipment. Brice, kill that light."

The night closed around them as the man obeyed. At the controls the driver was illuminated by the small gleams from ranked dials and the vehicle would be equipped with riding lights fitted beneath, but in the body there was nothing to reveal who was where. Dumarest moved, stooping to watch silhouettes against the star-brightened sky. Sayer hadn't moved. He grunted as Dumarest rose to stand beside him.

"Earl?"

"Yes. What happens now?"

"We go back to the station, check in the raft and gear."

"And?" Dumarest stepped to the man's rear as he made no answer. "What about me?"

"You'll be taken care of. A medical check first, a bath, some food and I guess you could do with a rest after what you've been through. Climbing to the roof like that was a crazy thing to do. Crazy!"

"You think so?"

"No doubt about it? What made you do it? If you'd just stopped for a minute to think you'd have realized there was no point in—" Sayer broke off as Dumarest clamped his left arm around his shoulders, lifted his right hand from his boot to the man's neck. "What the hell are you doing?"

"Feel this," said Dumarest softly. "It's a knife and it's resting against your windpipe. If you yell or struggle I'll cut your throat."

"You're insane!"

"Maybe." Dumarest looked at the man standing at the

searchlight, aside from the driver the only other occupant of the raft. "Take me to Charisse."

"If I don't?"

"You die," said Dumarest, and his tone left no doubt he meant it. "The man standing by the searchlight will go after you. The driver will do as I say once he sees you dead so it will all be the same in the end."

"Yes," said the old man. "I guess it will."

"Take me to Charisse."

"Now I know you're crazy. She won't see you. She's busy and you'll have to wait. In any case—" Sayer drew in his breath as a slight movement of the knife slit the skin at his throat. "All right, Earl! All right!" As Dumarest released him he dabbed at the smart, the blood. Looking at the smears on his fingers he said, "You bastard!" Then, to the driver, "Take us back to the house. Land in the inner court."

Chapter Eleven

She sat in a room ceilinged with shadows; gloom rested like a cloud so as to mask all detail ten feet above the carpeted floor. A trick of lighting as was the shimmering thing of crystal standing on a small table, the winking sparkles which came from flasks of restless fluids, the gleams which scintillated from her throat, the rich mane of her hair.

"Earl!" She rose to greet him, one hand resting on the table at which she'd been sitting, the scatter of papers spread over the polished wood. "My impetuous friend. All right, Dino, you may leave us."

"But—" He looked from one to the other. "Are you sure?"

"You think he will hurt me?" Her smile, her tone made a mockery of the concept. "I am as safe with him as with a hundred guards."

A confidence the old man didn't share and his hand crept up to touch the minor wound at his throat. The scratch had bled, the blood drying to leave an ugly smear, though she seemed unable to see it.

"Leave us," she said again, and this time her voice held impatience. "I assume you have no objection, Earl?"

"None."

"Then you may go." She waited until the door had closed on the old man and gently shook her head in mild reproof. "Such a devoted servant and so frail when compared to yourself. Did you have to threaten him? Cut the skin of his throat?" She leaned forward a little, eyes sparkling. "Would you really have killed him? Yes," she answered her own question. "Why not? Even though he had saved your life—why not? The law of the jungle, Earl; kill or be killed. Is that not so?"

He watched, saying nothing as she crossed the room to stand before the shimmering fabrication.

"Do you remember this?" It came alive beneath her touch, light flashing in motes and points of swirling brilliance which flared in silent explosions, to die, to be reborn in scintillant splendor. "My toy, Earl, surely you remember it? You saw it on Podesta when you acknowledged the debt you owed me. The small matter of having saved your life—but, now, that seems little to you. Would you have preferred me to have let you die? Your life, Earl, and not once but twice. A heavy debt for an honest man."

"Once," he said. "Not twice."

"Because you consider the original debt paid? The blood and tissue and sperm taken from your body sufficient compensation?" She smiled, then shrugged as if the matter were of no importance. "We will not argue the matter. Some wine?"

She moved to where a decanter stood with glasses and poured without waiting for his answer. As she turned, he strode toward the shimmering toy and, finding the switch, turned it off. As it darkened, the shadows thickening the upper reaches of the chamber seemed lower than before.

"Earl?"

"A distraction," he said. "One I can do without."

"So that you can concentrate on me?" She came toward him, one hand extended, the glass resting in her fingers. "Take it, Earl. Drink. At least let us share a toast to your continued good fortune." She sipped, frowning when he made no effort to follow her example. "Perhaps you would care to bathe first. Are you in pain?"

He was in too much pain for comfort but he ignored it as he did her suggestion. A shower had washed the pulp and

140

slime from his clothing, the blood from his face and neck and hands. One taken with Sayer an unwilling partner.

"You hesitate," she said. "You did not refuse when Linda Vyna made you the same offer. Did you enjoy her ministrations? Was the bitch gracious? At least she's had experience enough in entertaining men in need." She drank and lowered the empty glass. "Do you love her?"

"No."

"Yet you would use her. As you were willing to use me on Ascelius."

"To escape," he said. "And you were there to help me do it. A lucky coincidence."

"They happen."

"Perhaps."

"Have you never known others?" She refilled her glass and, when she turned, again she was smiling. "Come, Earl, why be so suspicious? Drink and relax and talk to me. Of your travels and other coincidences you have known. Surely there are some?"

"Many." He lifted his glass and lowered it untouched. Her eyes ignored its passage. "One should amuse you. Two brothers left home at various times to seek their fortunes. Both became mercenaries and, after twenty years, they met on a battlefield."

"And one killed the other?"

"I said they were mercenaries," he said patiently. "They had been at their trade long enough to have learned the futility of slaughter. One held the upper hand and made an offer; terms which would leave his opponents far less than what they had but more than they could hope to retain if beaten into submission. The offer was accepted."

"And when they met face to face and realized their relationship they joined forces and turned against those who had hired them?"

"No. Mercenaries, if nothing else, are realists. The terms stood but, afterwards, they traveled together. A mistake; while there was work for one there was not enough for two. Finally they argued over a woman and one killed the other. He lived barely long enough to claim his prize; she had loved the other and took her revenge in bed."

"So?" She frowned. "What is your point?"

"A simple one, Charisse. Things are not always what they

141

seem. You, for example, a young and beautiful woman—who would take you for a liar?"

She said, tightly, "You are a guest in my house, Earl. I suggest you remember that."

"A guest?" He looked at the glass in his hand then set it on the table. "On Podesta you told me your father had died a year earlier. I believed you—why should you bother to lie? But later I learned that a man, Rudi Boulaye, had visited you. You, Charisse, not your father. Circe was not a man. That was ten years ago."

"So? My father was busy."

"He would never have been too busy to entertain Boulaye. They shared a common interest. Did you see him?"

"Boulaye? No. I merely gave him access to the library and Armand's papers. He offered to pay and I had need of the money at that time." She drank some of her wine. "I wish you'd drink with me, Earl."

"Later, perhaps."

"It's harmless, I swear it." She shrugged as he made no comment. "All right, so I lied. What of it?"

"I wondered why. Was it just to make yourself seem younger than you are? A harmless vanity? But then came the meeting on Ascelius and your loving care." His left hand rose to touch his temple. "The implant you so generously gave me."

"Something to ease your pain," she said quickly. "A convenient form of medication."

"Which dulled my intellect and made me amiable and robbed the temporal lobe of a true awareness of time. Which is why I removed it. What else did it contain? A receptor for a stunner? Something you could activate to throw me into an artificial sleep? Why? Were you afraid of me?"

Her laughter rose in genuine amusement. "Afraid of you, Earl, of all men you are the one I trust most. You couldn't hurt me if you tried. As you couldn't hurt the creature I set you against. Those fools, Enrice and the rest, they thought you had no chance but they hadn't seen you fight the man-nek. It was stronger, taller, better equipped and more fearsome and you fought it to the point of death. Yet you ran from an overgrown girl. Do you know why?"

"Tell me."

"A simple thing, Earl, the color of her hair. Black hair like

142

mine, like that of the child you risked your life to save. Whom did she remind you of? A woman you had loved? A child you had lost?" She paused, waiting, shrugging when he made no answer. "Not that it matters. I had the clue and it was enough. The rest was a matter of routine."

Of suggestions whispered into his ear while he lay at her mercy in drugged unconsciousness. Hypnotic conditioning used as an elementary precaution could have cost him his life. Not from the female he had faced, the men set on the roof of the building would have prevented that, but there could have been others. Black-haired women with the urge to kill.

"No, Earl!" Her voice held command. "Don't be a fool!"

He looked at his hand, at the knife he had drawn, the blade reflecting shimmers as it amplified the nervous tension of his muscles.

"You hate me," she mused. "But you can't harm me. Classic conditions for developing a mind-ruining conflict. One aggravated by your recent exertions. Another classic example, this time of an exercise in utter futility. What did you hope to gain? What had you to fear? The only dangers you faced were of your own choosing." Her eyes widened as he stepped toward her, to halt with the knife lifted, the point aimed at her throat. "Earl!"

"I can't harm you," he said. "Remember?"

"The knife—"

"An illustration. The real point of the story I told you. Things are not always what they seem, true, but the moral wasn't that. It was to make the point that it is a mistake to jump to the wrong conclusion. A knife is a tool designed to cut and so you imagine I intend hurting you. But you know I can't do that so—"

She cried out as the blade lifted, caught at her necklace, tore it free to send it flying to the floor where it lay with gleaming, winking eyes. The strands in her hair followed to lie in an ebon tangle.

"No!" She backed, hands lifted to shield her face. "No, Earl! No!" And then, with sudden fury, "You bastard! You'll pay for what you've done!"

He saw the fall of her hand, the gleam as she drew metal from her waist, springing forward, knife raised as she aimed the weapon at his face. Metal clashed as he knocked it aside, a thin, high ringing which rose to die in fading murmurs as he tore the gun from her hand to send it after the gems.

"You attacked me," she said incredulously. "You could have killed me." Then, dully, "Well, Earl, do you like what you see?"

She was still as tall, the curves of her body taut against the fabric of her gown and, with her face hidden in shadow, she seemed much the same. Then as he looked Dumarest noted changes, a blurring which seemed to accelerate, a shifting and alteration as the last shreds of illusion vanished before the impact of harsh reality.

Charisse was grotesque.

Nothing is really ugly in the context of its environment; a spider, a slug, a snail all have the beauty of functional design, but Charisse was a woman and, as a woman, she was monstrous.

"Armand," she said dully. "My loving father. My creator. A fool who aspired to be a god. The egotistical bastard! May he rot in hell." She took the glass of wine Dumarest had poured for her, stared at him for a moment, drank and threw the delicate crystal to shatter in a glitter of shards. "And you, Earl—did you have to be so cruel?"

He said nothing, handing her more wine. This time after drinking, she did not hurl the glass to ruin.

Bitterly she said, "You know, I was a very pretty child. A living doll, they used to call me. A sweet creature who won the hearts of all who saw me. A success, Armand thought. The living proof of his genetic skill." Her hand shook as she looked at the glass. "A pretty child—who would think it now?"

Those blind who would make their judgment on her voice but none who could see. The thrust of the knife had torn the wig from her scalp leaving a naked skull, the false eyebrows and eyelashes adding to the clownish distortion of her face pocked with nodulated skin, flesh mounding over bone puffed, seamed, a parody of what a face should be, rendered even more bizarre by the cosmetics emphasizing the eyes, the mouth, the line of the jaw.

"Do I disgust you, Earl?"

"No," he said with sincerity. "Never that."

"You are kind but I suppose no one who has traveled a

144

you have could be other than tolerant. Others are not so generous." The empty glass in her hand reflected the light in a host of broken rainbows as she twirled it between her fingers. Clean, well-shaped fingers, the flesh smooth, undistorted as was the hand. "It's progressive," she explained as if guessing his thoughts. "A gene which held an unsuspected weakness. One added to the chromosome pattern to give me a useful talent. It turned into a bomb which exploded into biological nightmare when triggered by the hormones released during puberty. At first it was minor; a slight thickening of the skin coupled with a succession of small nodulations. Treatment seemed to cure the problem but it merely eradicated the symptoms for a while. Armand did what he could but it wasn't enough. Nothing I tried was enough. I was doomed to turn into a repulsive freak."

"But you found an answer."

"A protection, yes." She handed him the empty glass and watched as he refilled it. "How did you guess?"

"I was curious," said Dumarest. "I wondered why such an attractive woman should choose to wear such gems. And I remembered what I've learned from working in carnivals. Always there is the noise and the shine, the glitter and the movement. The beat of drums to dull the hearing, the wink and gleam of tinsel to draw the eye, shifts of light to distract, to break unwanted concentration. An art, Charisse, one you developed to an unusual extent. But you had more than just paint and hypnotic gems. The teleths?"

"You know," she said. "Damn you, man, you know too much. Who else would have seen through my subterfuge? Would have guessed at the drugs he'd been given? The conditioning? Guessed and known what to do to free himself of both. That's why you ran and kept on running, wasn't it? Risked your life for no obvious reason, killed, climbed, faced death on the roof." Lifting her glass she said, "Earl, I drink to a most unusual man!"

As she lowered the glass he said, quietly, "The teleths?"

"Armand's madness or a part of it. Yes, Earl, he wanted to give me telepathic ability. Instead all I gained was the power to make others respond to me in a protective manner. They saw me as an object of tender affection—even when I turned into a monster that attribute remained. With the help of art, as you called it, I managed to mask my real appearance."

Her manner now seemed incredible. Had he really held her naked in his arms? Kissed her? Felt the overwhelming tide of passion, the ecstasy he had known on Podesta? Had it been real or merely the product of hypnotic suggestion as he lay drugged on the couch, arms clutching the air, perhaps, his orgasm collected in a flask as she won sperm to add to her stores.

"Earl?"

"Nothing." He shook his head, remembering her ability, wondering as to its depth. "You spoke of Armand's madness. Did your father—"

"My creator," she interrupted. "I call him a parent for convenience only. The only one I had. He constructed the chromosome pattern, did what needed to be done and, when the attempt proved viable, turned me over to the care of an artificial womb. The first, he hoped, of endless millions, all cloned from my body. The reason I had to be female. The perfect woman as he saw perfection. The Supreme Mother of the human race." Her laughter rose, harsh, brittle. "The fool! He wanted to turn back the clock and breed the creatures he swore must have inhabited Earth."

"You—"

"I'm the result of his lunacy. He had the dream but I inherited the nightmare. Can you imagine what it is to be like this? To know that things can only get worse? It isn't a disease, you understand. Not a cancer which can be cut or burned away. It's a natural part of me as the color of your hair is of you, the color of your eyes. In ten years time it will have spread. In twenty I will be twice the bulk I am now and the epidermis will begin to harden. A decade later and I will be locked in a prison of inflexible living tissue. And then what? Shall I metamorphose into something even more strange and horrible?"

Dumarest said, "Did Armand intend that? For you to develop wings, for example?"

"If he did he didn't tell me."

"His papers? Surely he must have kept records. If you had the original pattern wouldn't it give you a clue?"

"Do you think I haven't checked? The man was insane and believed in legends. The records show a pattern but how can I be certain it's mine?"

"You could check," he urged. "The original could be

among Armand's private papers." And they would be in the library if anywhere at all. If he could get to them, the books and records stored in the room, to find the secret he had come to learn and then to leave while there was still time—if there was still time. Dumarest said, "It would be a beginning. If nothing else it could resolve a doubt. Try, Charisse—what have you to lose?"

He had expected an argument, instead he gained immediate cooperation. Setting down her glass, she moved to where her wig and gems lay gleaming on the floor. Stooping she donned them, careless of his presence, making small adjustments by touch. When she turned to face him again lights winked from her throat and hair, gleams which drew his eyes from the parody of her face. Even as he watched that face seemed to blur, to take on softer, more endearing lines—illusion backed by telepathic projection.

He looked at the gun in her hand, the bare floor where it had lain.

"A mistake, Earl," she said. "Not your first, but it's probably your last. Move and I'll burn your legs off at the knees."

The table was at his side, the glass of untouched wine resting on it like a lambent gem. It crashed to shatter in a pool of liquid as Dumarest upended the heavy board.

From behind it he said, "Remember, Charisse, the Cyclan won't pay you for a corpse."

The snout of the laser wavered, dropped from where it had aimed at his upper body. To carry out her threat the woman would have to burn through the wood and with such a light-weight weapon that would take time. Time for him to take action of his own. Yet should he move, expose his legs, she would fire.

A mistake as she had said; he should have remembered the gun, but he had been too eager to get to the library, to find the secret it could contain. But why had she threatened him at all? The answer lay in the hand she lifted to her face, the fingers touching the ornate wig. He had stripped her of defenses, exposing her true appearance and humbling her pride. To her, now, revenge would be sweet.

"Help," he said, talking to distract her attention, to ease the tension he felt mounting between them. If it rose too high not even her promised reward would keep her from closing her finger on the release. "They promised to help you. Is that why you contacted them?"

"Clever," she said. "You're too damned clever, but not this time. I didn't contact them, they got in touch with me. After Podesta when I'd taken what I wanted from you and was out in space. They thought you were riding with me and offered to buy you. A good price, Earl, too good for what you seemed to be and I became curious. What made you so special? You are fast and strong and intelligent but why should the Cyclan be interested in that? So I came after you."

To Ascelius and what else?

Dumarest was certain but it did not harm to talk, to continue easing the tension and so gain a measure of greater safety. Against an ordinary woman he would have taken a chance if there had been no other way, snatching out his knife and throwing it and trusting to speed and luck that it would strike home before the gun could be fired or, if fired, badly aimed. But Charisse had a degree of telepathic ability, enough to warn her of imminent danger, and she was almost hysterical with released fury. He saw the tautness of the skin over her knuckle, the white rim around the irises of her eyes. Anger blazing, barely contained, obvious despite the illusion.

He said, "And now you have me, Charisse. What did they offer? What do you hope to gain?"

"So much, Earl. So very much." Even the thought of it brought a degree of calm. The finger eased a little and the eyes lost some of their wild fixity. "The full resources of their laboratories to isolate and cure the malfunction built into my chromosome pattern. Money to enable me to continue my own research."

"Together with a few technicians to reside here with you to guide that research," he said. "The advice of the Cyclan at all times free of charge. Correct?"

"And if it is?"

"You'll become a servant of the Cyclan, Charisse. It will be inevitable. Within a few years you'll be totally dependent on them for your income if nothing else. And, always, they'll dangle the carrot of a final cure before your eyes." Dumarest took a step toward the edge of the table. Given time and a short enough distance he would make a rush to snatch the gun from her hand. Risking a burn for the sake of escape from the trap she had constructed. "But no cure will ever be discovered and you must know it. Don't be a fool, woman! Don't sell yourself for a lie! A promise which can't be kept!"

"Move again and I'll ruin your face." The laser rose to aim at his eyes. "I know where to hit, Earl, how deep to burn."

And how to heal should the need arise. Did she know that, to the Cyclan, only his brain was of value? The knowledge he held within it? The secret which they hunted as he sought to find the coordinates of Earth?

He said, "We could make a deal. Work to our mutual advantage. There is no need for you to hand me over to the Cyclan at all. In fact it would be a mistake. As you guessed, I'm valuable to them, and once you know why you'll have something to bargain with. They'll give you all you want and on your own terms. You tell them nothing until they deliver your cure. A new face," he urged. "An end to pretense. No more hiding behind a veil of illusion. No more fear of what is to come. Trust me, Charisse. Trust me."

The gun wavered a little, began to lower, the finger growing slack on the trigger as she digested his offer. He could almost read her mind, the computations she was making. To lie, promise him anything in order to learn why he was so valuable, then to lock him away as insurance while she made her arrangements with the Cyclan. A mouse dealing with a cat but she needn't know that. In the meantime he would make his own chances.

Dumarest tensed, ready to make his rush should she prove stubborn, to snatch at the weapon and negate its threat. Once that had been done he would promise anything to gain access to the library and the precious papers it would contain.

His plans shattered as brilliance winked from a point behind him. The guide beam of a laser accompanied by the burning shaft of raw energy which touched the woman's wrist, to spear it, to send her weapon falling as it cauterized the wound it had made.

Dumarest turned, hand freezing as he saw the tall figure, the aimed laser, the glow of scarlet and the gleam of the nated seal on the breast of the robe. The face which rose like a skull above the thrown-back cowl.

From where she stood the woman said, "Okos! Why did you fire? There was no need!"

The cyber from Ascelius—a man insane.

Chapter Twelve

There was beauty in madness. A burning, brilliant devastation of old restrictions and hampering patterns of thought. An opening of new dimensions of awareness and the appreciation of a vaster scope of achievement. Often while rising from rapport with those gifted brains in central intelligence he had experienced the ultimate in mental intoxication. An ecstasy he had never dreamed existed or could possibly exist. Even now he wasn't sure why, of all the servants of the Cyclan, he should have been chosen.

And yet it seemed so clear.

Despite their awesome intelligence the assembled brains depended on the use of men to execute their desires. Gifted men, trained, specially selected, but men just the same. And men held an ingrained weakness. Even the best must fall far short of the aspirations of those they were dedicated to serve. For long ages they had waited, hoping that their servants would rise to their needs and now, finally, they had decided to act.

The brains with whom he had been in direct contact. That part of central intelligence which had tested him and found him not wanting. Unhampered by established tradition. Unrestricted by artificial barriers.

Elge was wrong. The newly elected Cyber Prime was too cautious and, impatient, the brains had chosen him to take his place. Okos, Cyber Prime—the words had a ring like the throb of bells. And it could be done so easily. With the brains aiding him, no, showing him the need, all had become clear. Dumarest on Podesta. His prediction as to his movements— everything which had followed, all proved he should be the ultimate master. And now, aside from minor details, all was accomplished.

"You will remove the knife." Okos gestured with the laser. "Your left hand, first finger and thumb only, let it fall."

An inward glow as the man obeyed. As all would obey once he was the Cyber Prime. And soon, now. Soon.

"The woman is hurt," said Dumarest. "May I attend her?" A request he knew would be refused; one made only to gain her friendship. "No? Some wine, then? May I give her some wine?"

Poison to dull the intellect—why were these lesser beings such fools? Yet that same folly made them easy to manipulate. Greed and personal satisfaction and indifference to the welfare of others. A multitude would only be as strong as one. Cattle for harvesting—labor to build the new universe.

How clear it all was!

"Wine," said Dumarest. Then, to the woman, "You see how concerned your friends are about you? That shot could have taken off your hand. He could just as easily have sent it into your brain. Ask him why he didn't?"

Okos looked at her as she obeyed. "To kill you would be a waste. I may still require your assistance."

"And you hope to get it?" Her voice rose. "You scarlet swine I'll see you rot first!"

"To refuse aid will gain you nothing."

"I want only what you promised. The cure and—"

"The cure will be given you when it is discovered. The rest also as we agreed. I do not lie. The Cyclan does not lie." The tone was the careful modulation of all cybers but the words carried a chill. "Further argument is an illogical waste of time."

Was he alone? Dumarest looked around the chamber seeing nothing but a narrow panel, open, through which the

151

cyber had come. Had the guards who had chased him worked for him or the woman? Why had the cyber fired?

The answers to those questions could mean life or death.

Dumarest looked at the tall figure, the face, the eyes, the set of the mouth. All cybers looked gaunt and all radiated the aura of protoplasmic robots, but Okos was unusual. A man who seemed to be gloating over some secret joy—and no cyber could experience physical pleasure. The joy of achievement, then, of having made a successful capture, but why was he alone? Knowing his movements as Okos had known, it would have been simple to have taken him on Podesta. Yet he had been allowed to escape. Apparently escape—but why?

Madness had to be the answer.

Insanity as defined by a cyber.

The touch of human ambition and greed.

A guess but the only logical answer if the known facts were to fit. An unsuspected weakness in the man's character had revealed its flaw under the pressure of staggering opportunity.

Dumarest said, "Charisse, do you know why the Cyclan consider me to be so valuable? Would you like me to tell you?"

"Silence." Okos lifted the laser. "You will remain silent."

"I have a secret," continued Dumarest. "One stolen from a Cyclan laboratory a long time ago. A biological chain consisting of fifteen units which enables an intelligence to—"

Smoke rose from the table beneath the touch of the laser's beam. It sent more smoke rising an inch from Dumarest's boot.

"You will remain silent or I will burn your vocal chords," said Okos. "The woman must not be told."

"Why not? What harm can it do? You will kill her anyway."

"Kill me?" Charisse lifted her arm, stared at the blackened wound, then at the cyber. "Okos! You promised!"

"You will not be harmed if he keeps silent."

"Look at your wrist if you believe that," said Dumarest. "His token of friendship. Do you know why he burned you? Ask him. He'll tell you it was because he feared you might fire and kill me. Or fire and kill him if we had made a deal. As he would still fire if I told him we had. Shall I prove it?"

"No!" She looked again at her wrist. "No!"

She believed him and Dumarest knew he had managed to drive a wedge into their mutual trust. Knew too that he held her life in his hand. Two words would do it. All he need say to the cyber was "She knows."

Okos would do the rest.

But how to get rid of the cyber in turn?

Dumarest had the advantage of being physically safe as far as a threat to his life was concerned. His value lay in what he knew; the correct sequence of the fifteen units forming the affinity twin. The biological entity which enabled the dominant partner to take over the mind and body of a subjective host. Literally to become that host. With it Charisse could live and act and love and feel and be a young and lovely girl. The reflection she would see in her mirror would be that of the selected host.

Cybers could become the rulers of worlds and knit them into the common plan.

Okos could become the Cyber Prime.

That was the chance he had seen and taken—there could be no other explanation for his actions. The Cyclan had contacted Charisse. After learning he was not aboard why hadn't they concentrated on Podesta?

"I directed them to Quen," said Okos when Dumarest bluntly put the question. "The predictions were of almost equal probability that you could be on there or Ascelius."

And, as he hadn't been reported on Ascelius, they had directed their agents to look elsewhere. But Okos had known and had chosen to retain his knowledge.

The madness which would save him.

Dumarest said, "The coincidence of Charisse's ship? Arranged, I assume?"

"There was no coincidence. From the moment you set foot on Ascelius you were under constant observation. Used, hunted, driven like the animal you are to take the path I chose. It suited my plans to allow you freedom of movement until it was time to end the farce."

"The time in jail," said Dumarest. "Held while you waited for Charisse to arrive. Followed then attacked so as to be rescued." He added, bleakly, "Did Myra Favre have to die?"

An answer he knew; one way or another she had been doomed. Had she not fallen the wine would have killed her and the end would have been the same. He felt a renewed anger against the Cyclan, the organization which treated people as if they were pieces to be moved on a board. Things devoid of needs or feelings. Expendable pawns used in a game of conquest.

He controlled his anger—if he were to live he needed to be calm.

He looked at the woman. The illusion had slipped a little, the pain of her wound taking priority so that her face looked softened as if made of wax. A potential ally and the only one he had. But how to win her aid?

Okos provided the answer. He stepped forward, tall, arrogant, conscious of his power. Already the universe was his. Eyes, deep-sunken beneath ridged brows, stared with a burning intensity.

"You will arrange transportation," he told the woman. "I shall also need restraints and medication. Your own vessel will serve."

"A servant," said Dumarest. "Too bad, Charisse, but I did warn you."

"It is a privilege to serve the Cyclan," said Okos. "Obey if you hope for reward."

"And keep hoping." Dumarest moved to lean casually against the upended table. "What's the matter with your own acolytes, Okos? Did they turn against you when they realized you'd gone mad?" A guess but a good one and he tensed, gambling enough sanity remained for Okos to hold his fire. A risk taken and a gamble won and he was sure now the cyber was alone. "He needs you, Charisse," he said. "But once he's got what he asked for he'll kill you. If you don't realize that you're a fool. I suggest you do something about it."

"Remain silent." Okos leveled the weapon in his hand. "I shall not warn you again."

"Earl—"

"You too, woman." The laser moved a little, halted. "Must I teach you another lesson?"

She screamed as the laser fired, flame bursting from the mass of ebon hair, the wig catching, smoking, burning as she tore it from her head. The winking gems flared and died, robbed of life by the savage blast, only those at her throat struggling to maintain the illusion. A wasted effort and her parody of a face twisted in rage at the affront to her pride.

"You bastard, Okos! You'll pay—"

154

Again he fired, smoke rising from her shoulder, her scream echoed by something from above. A black shape which dropped from the clustered shadows to swing on a line of silk, to poise, to drop with scrabbling claws and gnashing mandibles on the head of the cyber.

A mutated spider set to keep the area free of other life forms, a guardian, an observer—a thing now wild with ravening fury.

Okos reared, his free hand tearing at the creature which covered his head and face. Blood ran in thick streams beneath the scrabbling limbs, staining the scarlet with a deeper carmine, dripping on the floor as, wildly, he fired and fired again.

Dumarest flung himself down, reached for his knife, lunged forward with it in his hand, the edge rising, touching, tearing through the flesh and bone of the wrist to send the hand and laser flying to one side. Blood fountained to join the rest, more following as he stabbed, the blade driving between the ribs into the heart. As the cyber fell the scrabbling shape rose, running back up its silk to hide and lurk in shielding darkness.

"Earl!" Charisse had been hit, blood welling from between the fingers she clasped to her side. The wound on her shoulder showed charred bone, that on her wrist had started to bleed. "Help me, Earl."

She was dying and knew it. She stared into his face as he knelt, shaking her head as he tried to examine her side.

"Leave it, Earl. The bastard got me."

"I'll call someone. Sayer—he could help."

"He could keep me alive, maybe," she corrected. "But alive for what? I don't want to be a freak, Earl. It's better this way. But call him. Tell him to help you clear up the mess. He's a good man. He'll—" She gulped and, with sudden clarity, said, "Earl. On Podesta. When we—did you love me then?"

"I loved you."

"You're a good liar, Earl." Her hand fell away to be stained by a gush of blood. "A good—"

"Charisse?"

She made no answer. She was dead.

Dino Sayer snuffled and touched his throat and said, "She was good in her way, Earl. I'll miss her."

"But not me?"

"No." The man was honest. "You've given me enough to remember you by. And I can't help but think if she hadn't met you she'd be alive now. Well, that's the way it goes. If it were left to me—but you won the wager and I guess you've earned the right." He gestured at the door. "The library. You'll find everything indexed. Armand's papers are in the end file. If you want anything just press the bell. It's at the side of the desk."

The room was filled with the scent of moldering paper, dust, dank air, neglect, creeping decay. The ubiquitous shadows masked whatever might be lurking in the molding running beneath the ceiling, but if any existed they would be harmless. As would be any eavesdropping devices such as Charisse had fitted to the bedrooms. How else had she known of his interlude with Linda Ynya? How better to gain an idea of distrust or need?

A woman tormented, who had played with fire and had been burned, and had paid the price of having trusted the deranged cyber.

Later he would think about Okos and what his condition had revealed. Now there was work to be done.

Dumarest made his way to the shelves, searched, found books which he placed on the desk. A lamp threw a brilliant cone of light over stained and mottled pages blurred beneath their protective coatings of transparent plastic. Lists of supplies, journeys made by ancient vessels, annotations in various hands, names underlined or scored through, neat symbols made with mathematical precision. Many of the pages bore obviously recent markings on the plastic made with a pointed instrument.

A wealth of rare and ancient treasure, logs, reports, surveys, assessments, journals, the whole needing months of careful sifting—but Rudi Boulaye's visit had been short.

Dumarest put aside the heap and moved to the file. Armand had been a methodical man and would have condensed essential data while eliminating duplication and irrelevancies. The file opened to reveal neatly stacked folders each carefully marked with an abstract symbol.

Armand had known what they represented—Dumarest did not.

He took the first and rifled the sheets, recognizing computer read-outs based on logic-illogical forms of reference. Typed notes showed that various legends had been tested for message, simplicity and repetitive factors. Whoever had done the valuation had been thorough; children's bedtime stories had been included. The conclusions were what he'd expected; a legend could be a message from one generation to posterity in which case it needed to be short, simple and repetitive. Groundwork covered and cleared in a scientific manner and leading to what?

Another file listed stories of a fabulous nature but dealing with beasts and societies and not worlds. Another dealt with the apparent paradox of many diverse types existing simultaneously on a single planet, the chances of spontaneous development and the potential stress factors involved when opposed and diverse cultures met in a limited environment. The conclusion was that there would be inevitable warfare.

A study of the effects of an alteration in solar emission on an inhabited world.

A valuation of the amount of shipping which would be needed to evacuate the peoples of a planet with a population twice that normally to be found on an industrial world.

An assessment of the probable effects of induced aversion hysteria as applied to an entire section of the human race.

Nowhere could he find mention of Earth.

"My lord?" The girl who answered his pressure on the button had a round face now marked by recent tears. Grief for her dead mistress echoed in the wide band of black worn on her left bicep. A custom Dumarest had seen before.

He said, "Did Armand have any other files? A special book or something like it?"

"I don't know, my lord."

"Who would?"

"Perhaps the new master, my lord. Do you want to see him?"

He arrived thirty minutes later, again touching his throat at the sight of Dumarest, a reactive gesture he probably wasn't aware he made.

"You've been promoted," said Dumarest. "Allow me to congratulate you."

157

"Someone had to run the place." Dino Sayer shrugged, unimpressed by his new position. "Trouble?"

"I can't find what I'm looking for." Dumarest gestured at the files, the assembled records. "There must be another way. Do you remember Rudi Boulaye? He visited here about ten years ago." Dumarest continued at the other's nod. "Did he stay long."

"Not as I remember."

"How long?" Dumarest pursed his lips at the answer, the time had been less than he'd estimated, but it proved what he suspected. "He didn't see Charisse, right? Then who took care of him?"

"Octen. He's dead now."

"He had access to Armand's files?"

"Yes." Sayer frowned, thinking. "Now I come to think of it he had a lot of stuff in his room. Books, recordings, things like that. Files too, I think. One for sure which Armand used to keep by him and which Octen must have borrowed and forgotten to return."

"Where is it now?"

"Probably burned with the rest of his stuff." Sayer looked at the hand Dumarest had closed around his arm, the savage set of his mouth. "Something wrong?"

"The file. Can you make sure it's gone? It was the personal property of Armand and so could have been saved. The file, man. The file!"

The one Boulaye must have seen. The one Octen had neglected to replace in the cabinet. Papers which could hold the answer now perhaps lying moldering in some forgotten corner.

Alone in a small room Dumarest paced the floor forcing himself to be calm. Sayer had promised to do his best but time was running out. Soon it would be sunset and Linda Ynya would have left along with her ship and the passage she had offered and which he had to take. To delay was to risk being made the prisoner of the Cyclan. If that happened there would be no escape now Charisse was dead.

"Here!" Sayer was back, a folder held in his hand. "This could be it. I had to search the stores and was lucky to find it." As Dumarest snatched it his tone softened a little. "I guess it's important to you, eh?"

"Yes."

"Maybe I was too harsh blaming you for what you did."
Again the hand lifted to the small cut on the puckered skin
of his neck. "But when you've just saved a man's life and he
threatens to cut your throat—well, that isn't an easy thing to
forget."

Dumarest said, "Just give it time. Now if you'll let me read
this?"

The papers were closely covered with neat script; headings,
paragraphs, summations, conclusions. Too much to read and
too much to scan. Too much even to have copied in the time
available. Already the sun was close to the horizon and, from
the field, came the echo of a warning siren. But, somewhere
in the folder, must be the answer Boulaye had found.

The whereabouts of Earth.

The coordinates he had risked his life to find.

From the riffled pages a dead man whispered via the
printed word; Armand forwarding a message, the fruit he had
found, the secret—". . . so in conclusion it appears obvious
that the supposedly mythical world known as Earth was far
from that and, in fact, could still exist. According to the story
told by the Erce sect on Newdon, Earth is to be found in a
region where stars are few and in a position from which certain patterns identified by names such as Leo, Libra and
Cancer are to be found. There are twelve such patterns which
must be arrangements of stars, or constellations, as seen from
the planet."

A thing Dumarest had already learned. Impatiently he
flipped the pages.

". . . which leads us to the inevitable conclusion that
Earth, or Terra as it is sometimes called, must lie within the
region bounded by the patch of dust lying to the galactic
north of Silus, the energy pool known as Morgan's Sink to
the galactic west of Crom, and the Hygenium Vortex. These
areas give the parameters as specified by the Erce sect and
while the names may have become distorted by the passage
of time the coordinates have not. They are alien to our
present system but that is to be expected if, at one time,
Earth's primary was considered to be the navigational center
of the galaxy. The revised and adjusted coordinates which
now give the exact position of Earth are. . . ."

The rest of the page was missing.

"Earl?" Sayer backed from Dumarest's expression. "God, man, what's wrong? You look like murder."

He felt it—but Boulaye was long dead. Boulaye who had ripped the page across and had taken the relevant portion to make certain that no one else would learn the secret.

Dumarest wished him screaming in hell!